THE
GO-for-GOLD
GYMNASTS

Reaching
HIGH

Previous books in the Go-for-Gold Gymnasts series

Winning Team

Balancing Act

THE
GO-for-GOLD
GYMNASTS

Reaching HIGH

by DOMINIQUE MOCEANU
and ALICIA THOMPSON

DISNEP • Hyperion Books
New York

Printed in the United States of America
First Edition
10 9 8 7 6 5 4 3 2 1
V475-2873-0 12131

Library of Congress Cataloging-in-Publication Data

Moceanu, Dominique, 1981–
   Go-for-gold gymnasts: reaching high/by Dominique Moceanu and Alicia
Thompson.—1st ed.
      p. cm.—(The go-for-gold gymnasts; bk. 3)
   Summary: Just before freshman year, Jessica, the quiet girl on the Texas
Twisters, surprises her teammates by going out for the cheerleading squad.
   ISBN 978-1-4231-3657-6 (alk. paper)
   [1. Gymnastics—Fiction. 2. Cheerleading—Fiction. 3. Friendship—
Fiction. 4. Competition (Psychology)—Fiction. 5. Teamwork (Sports)—
Fiction. 6. Family life—Texas—Fiction. 7. Houston (Tex.)—Fiction.]
I. Thompson, Alicia, 1984– II. Title.
   PZ7.M71278Gor 2012
   [Fic]—dc23   2011041624

Designed by Tyler Nevins
Text is set in 13 point Minion Pro.

Visit www.disneyhyperionbooks.com

To all of you who are facing adversity—
keep pressing forward, because the rewards
for your loyal dedication are certain to be
nothing short of spectacular.
—D. M.

For August
—A. T.

One

Do you know how awesome it feels to have a parade thrown just for you? What it's like to wave toward the sidelincs at little girls on their fathers' shoulders, who are cheering because of something *you* did, an accomplishment that means so much not just to you, but to your family and your friends and your entire hometown?

Yeah, me neither.

Technically, I was on the float, and I was wearing a cheesy red-white-and-blue dress, and my cheeks hurt from smiling. But the parade wasn't for me—it was for my teammate Britt, who had won a medal on the vault at the Junior National Championships, and it was for my teammate Christina, who had won a medal on the bars and placed in the top ten all around, and most especially it was for my teammate Noelle, who was the number five gymnast in the country and the gold medalist on the balance beam.

I hadn't competed at the Junior National Championships a week ago, because I hadn't qualified. To be completely honest, I hadn't even tried out, because I wasn't an Elite gymnast yet and so wasn't able to compete in the higher-level competitions. I'd missed my chance to make the team last spring, and now I'd have to wait several months before getting another chance.

Someday, I vowed, I'd get onto a float like this on my own. But today wasn't that day.

Britt nudged me. "Are these dresses pure polyester?" she asked, pulling the itchy collar away from her neck. I knew it must be itchy, because it was the exact same scoop neckline that my dress had, and it was all I could do not to tug at it with the hand I wasn't using to wave to my adoring public. Well, my teammates' adoring public, anyway.

"I thought they stopped using that stuff in the seventies," I said.

"They should've *outlawed* it," Britt said. "Especially on a Texas afternoon in early August. I wish they would've let us wear our team leotards. At least I'd be cooler."

As hot as I was—and it was sweltering outside, so hot that I kept waving partly just to keep sweat from pooling under my armpit—there was no way I'd have felt comfortable wearing only a leotard in front of a crowd like this. On the competition floor it was different. You weren't focused on everyone looking at you; you were too busy worrying about the judges; that switch leap in your first dance series that had been tripping you up in practice; and your competitor's score, which was flashing just out of your line of sight, with you thinking, *don't look don't look don't look*, though you could see her hugging her coach, and you knew she'd done well, maybe even better than you could do. But out here, I was on display. And while I felt kind of stupid in this ridiculous dress, at least I didn't feel exposed.

We took the last turn of the circuit, ending in front of the Texas Twisters gym, where we all trained six days a week. There was a huge banner across the front of it, congratulating the Elite girls on their accomplishments. I felt like an actress attending an awards ceremony where I hadn't been nominated for anything. I could sit and listen to the speeches, but it didn't mean I'd go home with a little golden statue.

"Do you think they'll throw another parade if we win something at the international meet?" Christina asked. "Or will they be, like, we just threw them a parade, so we're not going to do another one?"

"The meet's in October," Britt pointed out. "So at least it will be cooler then. I mean, not that the parade would be for me, or anything."

Both Christina and Noelle had made the National team on the basis of their all-around scores at the Junior National Championships, which meant they had a chance to compete at a camp and earn a spot at the USA vs. the World event. But although Britt had competed at the Junior Nationals and come home with an individual medal, she'd hurt her ankle in the all-around competition and so had placed out of contention to go to the camp. Still, at least she'd had a shot. I'd watched the entire thing from the stands.

"Maybe it'll rain," I muttered.

Only Britt heard me, and she grinned. "Hey, that's clever," she said. "Raining on a parade, ha-ha."

"Of course, I hope it doesn't," I said quickly.

I didn't want Britt to think I was bitter, because really, I wasn't. Christina had the most beautiful, graceful lines I'd ever seen, and Noelle had worked so hard and dealt with so much stress to get to Nationals, I couldn't be anything but happy for them. This international competition was between China, Romania, and Russia and us, and it was meant to be like a fun preview of the Olympics. It would even be on TV, although they'd probably show the Senior girls more than the Junior side of the competition. Still, it would be cool.

Most of the time, you could count on Britt to say something funny, something that would lighten the mood and make you laugh and distract you from whatever you might be dwelling on. But now all she said was, "I know you didn't mean anything bad," as she watched Noelle alight from the float and join her family, who were waiting to wrap her up in a hug.

I was careful stepping down from the float myself, because I was wearing platform sandals that were hand-me-downs from my stepsister, Tiffany, and didn't fit me that well. I was paying so much attention to not twisting my ankle that I almost ran right into the man standing at the bottom of the float.

"Whoa, there, Tiger," he said. I looked up, because there was only one person in the world who had ever called me that.

I hadn't expected to see him there, and I threw my arms around him instinctively. "Dad! What are you doing here?"

"My favorite daughter is being honored in a parade," he said in his Texas drawl. "Where else do you think I should be?"

At work. On vacation in the Cayman Islands. Visiting my stepmonster's family in Vermont. Getting new hardware installed on the doors in his house.

These were all of the excuses I'd heard recently for why he hadn't been able to make it to my last competition, or why he couldn't come to the weekly therapy sessions I was forced to have now, or why he couldn't take me camping like he'd promised. But I decided not to think about it too much; it was nice to have him here this time, no matter what.

"I'm your *only* daughter," I reminded him, giggling. This was an old routine we'd done since I was four years old. "So how can I be your favorite?"

"That's tricky," he said. "Why don't we debate it over some finger food? I saw pigs in a blanket inside." He looked uncomfortable for just a second, so brief I almost missed it. My father was one of Austin's top news anchors; he'd reported out of a shelter the summer of the bad hurricanes, and he never got flustered. "I'm allowed to say that, aren't I, Tiger? Pigs in a blanket?"

"Sure," I said awkwardly. "That's what they're called, right? Hot dogs and cheese in a pastry thing?"

"Right," he said. "I didn't know if I was allowed to say that with . . . you know. Your mother says you're in therapy."

My cheeks burned as I realized what he was getting at. Only a few months before, I'd entered a treatment program to help with my eating disorder. I felt like I was making a lot of progress, but everyone acted like I was a time bomb waiting to explode if they used words like *food* or *weight* or *calories* in the wrong combination.

My mom approached us, and she had that tight smile that she wore when telemarketers called.

"Hi, honey," she said, leaning down to engulf me in a hug. When she straightened up, she said tersely, "Hello, Mark. Good of you to make it. Where's Vicki?"

"My favorite daughter is being honored in a parade," he said, repeating word for word what he'd said to me earlier. He didn't acknowledge my mom's question about his new wife. "I wouldn't miss it."

I could see written on my mother's face her memories of the countless events he'd missed over the years, and I willed her not to say anything to spoil this occasion.

Maybe the telepathy worked, because all she did was pull me close to her and say, "Well, it's so exciting. I still have this picture in my head of you when you were little, doing floor routines in our living room. Do you remember that? We had that big rug, and you used it for a floor mat, and you would turn somersaults and spin around to an eighties music compilation. That was the theme of your seventh birthday, practically—you showing off your gymnastics for all your friends."

I remembered it, too. It was weird to think that there'd been a time when I used gymnastics as something to impress people at school. The other girls loved it when I flipped around on the monkey bars at the playground, or turned a cartwheel when the teacher wasn't looking. Now sometimes, it felt like my sport was a state secret, and the less my peers knew about what I was doing, the better.

"Abracadabra,'" I said.

She leaned back to look at me, as if checking to see if my face was flushed with fever. "I'm sorry?"

"That's the song I would do my routine to," I reminded her. "It was called 'Abracadabra.'"

"That's right." She smiled, lost in reminiscence. "And now, to think that you're only five years away from possibly competing in an Olympics. It's unbelievable."

In fact, I couldn't believe it, but not because it was so amazing and incredible. It just seemed very unlikely.

"Speaking of which . . ." my father said, but he was addressing me, not my mother. "Jessie, would you mind coming with me outside? The film crew is here and would love to feature you for a spot on Channel Thirteen."

"Oh, Mark," my mother said, "I should've known. You're here for *work*?"

"I'm here for my *daughter*," he said stiffly,

correcting her. "But yes, I work for one of the main news outlets in the state, and I happen to have a very newsworthy daughter. Can I help it if my public might be interested in such a talented young lady?"

"Your public?" my mom sneered. Out of the corner of my eye, I saw my stepfather, Rick, approaching, apparently thinking that my mother needed some help. "You are so pompous some-times—"

"Stop!" I said. I could count on one hand the number of times my parents had been in the same room together since their divorce, and now I could see why. "I'll do it, okay? It's not a big deal."

"That's my Tiger," my dad said, smiling down at me. "Perhaps you could grab your friends, too? The one with the ponytail won a gold medal, right?"

"Sure," I said, trying to avoid my mother's gaze. Rick was at her elbow now, and I knew he would calm her down. "I'll meet you outside."

I set down my plate, which was stacked with food I hadn't actually touched, and went in search of my teammates. Christina wasn't hard to convince; as soon as she heard she'd be on TV, she'd made a beeline for the bathroom to check her hair.

Noelle looked uncertain—I knew she hadn't been totally thrilled at being featured on the news before the championships, when another reporter from Channel 13 had done a piece on us. But finally, she went to tell her mom and promised to be outside in five minutes. Britt was the only one who took some persuading.

"So, that's your dad?" she asked, craning her neck to see him still standing, arguing with my mother.

"You've seen him on TV before," I said peevishly. "Come on, let's just get this over with."

"He looks ruddier in person," she said. "Must be the makeup they have him wear for TV."

Britt used the weirdest words sometimes.

"Ruddier?" I said.

"Yeah: redder. What, public school doesn't teach vocabulary anymore?" Britt was homeschooled by her grandmother and never hesitated to remind us of how much more well-rounded her education was because of it. "I guess I'll find out soon enough," she added cryptically. "Look, if you don't want to do an interview, then don't do it."

I wanted to tell her that I knew what *ruddier* meant, I'd just been surprised to hear her say it.

I wanted to tell her that the last thing I was up to discussing just then was gymnastics, given that I wasn't even sure I deserved to be there.

I settled for heaving a big sigh. "Are you coming or not?"

Outside, there was a white news van with CHANNEL 13 painted across it in huge letters. My dad must've really planned this whole thing.

There was a lady who told us all where we should stand, and once we had our places, my dad emerged from the gym. I could tell, when he got closer, that he'd put a little makeup on, because his cheeks had a cakey quality to them. I was torn between hoping that my friends didn't notice this embarrassing detail and wondering why he hadn't offered me something to cover up my freckles.

"Okay," he said. "You girls smile big now, all right?"

He turned his back to me so he was facing the camera, and the cameraman gave the signal that they were rolling.

"You may not recognize me away from the anchor desk, but this is Mark Ivy with Channel Thirteen News, doing a very special field assignment. My daughter is one of four gymnasts being honored today at a parade here in downtown Austin, along with . . ."—I saw him glance down at an index card hidden discreetly in his palm—". . . Christina Flores, bronze medalist; Britt Morgan, silver medalist; and Noelle Onesti, who finished in the top five all around and won a gold medal on the balance beam."

Now he was thrusting the microphone toward us, and I froze. I wished I had thought to ask what kinds of questions he would throw at us. I didn't want to come across as being stupid if I stuttered over the answer.

But I didn't need to worry, because first, he leaned in toward Noelle, giving her a big smile that showed his teeth. "Noelle, how does it feel to win a gold medal at the Junior National Championships?"

Noelle tucked a strand of hair behind her ear. "It feels really good," she said. I didn't know if I was still on camera, and my cheeks were aching from smiling.

"Well, I know I speak for all of Austin when I say that we are so proud of you," my dad said. "All of you." He inclined his head toward the four of us, and even though my gaze was on him the whole time, he never glanced at me specifically. His face held its expression for just a moment too long, almost as if someone had paused the tape, and then the cameraman gave a thumbs-up.

"We got it," he said.

"Excellent," my dad replied, his face finally relaxing after that frozen smile. "Thank you, girls. Enjoy the rest of your party."

Noelle, Christina, and Britt split off and headed back inside, but I stayed behind. "Is that it?" I asked. "Are you leaving?"

My dad rumpled my hair. I'd sprayed it before I left the house with some smoothing serum of my mom's, and so I hoped that it wasn't springing around my head like a halo in the Texas heat. "Sorry, Tiger," he said. "I have to get back."

It was only after I watched him get into his sports car and drive away that I realized he'd never said why he had to go, or what was more important than this moment. I realized he'd never told me he was proud of *me*, his daughter. I realized that in his twenty-second news piece, I was the only one he'd never even mentioned by name.

Two

"**S**o, I heard you were in a parade." Dr. Fisher smiled at me. This was one of her therapist tricks—rather than ask a question, she would make a statement and expect you to elaborate. In my head, I planned on holding out and not saying anything at all, to *make* her ask a question. But I always caved.

Today was no different. "It was hot," I said. "Did you go?"

She hesitated. "No," she said, pursing her lips. "But I'm sure it was nice."

There was probably some rule in the therapist handbook that said, *You must not support your* clients by attending any function in their honor. Well, I could've told Dr. Fisher that she didn't need to worry—it hadn't been in my honor in the first place.

I was supposed to see Dr. Fisher every week as part of my treatment. Once, she'd asked me to draw an outline of what I thought my body looked like, and then we'd talked about how I was perceiving myself as fat when really I should have been able to see that I was a normal, healthy girl. Other than that, though, we didn't talk much about my eating behaviors or the way I used to make myself throw up sometimes to keep my weight down. Instead, we talked about other stuff, like gymnastics, and how much pressure it was, and even my dad. I didn't see why we focused on those things when I was supposed to be seeing her because of the eating thing, but in a way I was relieved.

I considered telling Dr. Fisher about the way my dad had shown up at the parade, done a news story about us, and then left, but I decided not to. I didn't know what she'd say about it.

"School starts up soon," I said instead.

"That must be exciting for you," Dr. Fisher said. "Or perhaps not, with all the homework."

She smiled again at me, and I could see a spot of lipstick where her top teeth met her gums. I knew that she was trying to relate to me, trying to let me know that she understood how hard it must be to be a teenage girl and have hours of homework. What she didn't get was that homework was the *least* of my worries.

"Yeah" was all I said.

"Are any of your friends in your classes?" she asked; I took this as a victory. An actual question!

"No." I frowned. "Actually, this is my first year of high school. Noelle and Christina will be in eighth grade, and Britt is a year behind them. She's home-schooled, anyway."

"Those are your gym friends," Dr. Fisher said, to clarify things, although I doubted she needed to by now. I'd talked about them enough, and even if she hadn't gone to the parade, she might've read the write-up in the paper about the three girls who went to the Junior National Championships. "But what about your school friends?"

For a second I just blinked at her, literally speechless. She might as well have been my Spanish teacher, asking me if Juan would like an orange or a yellow hat. I had no idea what she was talking about. I didn't think I'd ever had any school friends, since . . . well, since I could remember.

I knew better than to say that to Dr. Fisher, though. She'd have started making some of her comments about how tough that would be, or how lonely I must be, and I didn't know what I'd say in response.

"I've never needed anyone else," I blurted out. "Christina and Noelle have been my best friends since forever, and even though Britt just moved here earlier this year, we're really close. She's the one who . . ." I flushed. "Well, you remember."

"Mmm, I do remember," Dr. Fisher said. And then, because I knew she wouldn't let me get away with not explaining it, she said, "She was the one who turned you in to your coach, right?"

"Yeah," I said, "but I'm not mad about that anymore. I mean, I would've loved to have competed at the Elite qualifier, and then maybe at the Junior National Championships . . . but I know that she did what she thought she had to do."

"She sounds like a good friend," Dr. Fisher said softly. "I'm not suggesting you get rid of Britt, or any of the girls. But Britt is in seventh grade. Perhaps it would be nice to have other friends—girls your own age, girls with interests outside of gymnastics."

I tried to imagine what I would talk about with girls like that. I couldn't talk about makeup, because I only knew about the kind of lipstick that would give some definition to your face without appearing garish to the judges, but not about the lip gloss that might attract boys. I definitely couldn't talk about boys. There were some guys who trained at our gym, the kind of muscular, floppy-haired guys I figured the average girl would find cute. But to me, they were immature kids who were still in the lowest levels, barely competing routines where they got to pick their own music or moves. It was hard for me to picture myself having a crush on any of them.

"Think about it," Dr. Fisher said.

The envelope came on a Tuesday afternoon. I was home for my two-hour lunch break from gym before I had to go back for nighttime practice.

Technically, it was addressed "To the parents of Jessica Marie Ivy," but I opened it anyway.

Open house at Birchbark High School was in less than a week, and my class schedule was enclosed. I had Biology first period, followed by homeroom, then American Government, Algebra II, English I, and finally, P.E., for my last period.

Having P.E. at the very end of the day was highly desirable for several reasons, not the least of which was that then you didn't have to stink like sweaty socks for the rest of your classes, but I'd specifically requested P.E. as my first morning class. Ever since I'd started training seriously in gymnastics, I'd had P.E. in the morning, so that I could wake up at five o'clock, be at the gym by six, and have three hours to work out before I had to go to my first real class. I got a workout that was better than playing flag football, and I didn't have to wear the ugly gym uniform. Somehow, my schedule this year had gotten messed up.

That shouldn't be hard to fix, though, I thought. At that point, I was more concerned about whether I'd gotten good teachers or drawn the ones who were known to be strict or boring or crazy.

I went into the den, where Tiffany was draped over the leather couch, watching some reality TV show. I waited until there was a commercial break, so she wouldn't be mad at me for making her miss anything—even though, in my opinion, there wasn't much to miss. So far, the program seemed to be about a bunch of girls who all had the same bleached-blond hair competing for some guy who was famous twenty years ago.

"Hey, Tiff?" I said, perching on the edge of the couch. Tiffany was fifteen and about to be a sophomore, so she would know all about my teachers. She was also my incredibly moody step-sister, who'd bitten my head off before for asking her whether she wanted me to pass the mashed potatoes at dinner. It had been something about the tone of my voice, apparently.

"What?" she asked laconically. The TV was still tuned to the same channel, but she had pulled up the cable guide and was scrolling through it, probably looking for another crappy reality show.

"I got my schedule for next year, and I was wondering—"

Tiffany's eyes lit up as if someone had turned on a switch, and she jumped to her feet. "Where's the mail?" she asked. "Did mine come? Why didn't you bring it to me?"

"It's on the counter," I said. "You were busy. I was wondering—"

Tiffany brushed past me, and I followed her into the kitchen, where she began sorting through the mail strewn across the granite kitchen island. She ripped into her envelope, letting its shreds fall to the floor as she eagerly scanned the contents.

I glanced down at my own letter. "I have Smith for Biology," I said, reading off the first name on the schedule. "Do you know if she's nice? Or is it a he?"

"How would I know?" Tiffany sneered, even though she'd just finished her freshman year at the very same high school.

"So, that's a new teacher?" I asked. "What about Freeman for American Government, then?"

Tiffany had slid her cell phone out of her pocket and was punching in numbers, still clutching her class schedule in one hand. "He's good," she said, but in a dismissive way, as though she hadn't actually been listening.

"Is his class interesting?"

She rolled her eyes at me as she held her phone to her ear. "What does it matter? You'll take home all the work and spend your days in the gym instead." She brightened once someone on the other end picked up. "Oh, my God, did your schedule come in the mail? Who'd you get?" Then she disappeared into her bedroom, slamming the door behind her.

I stared down at the sheet of paper in my hand. I guess I should've been relieved—Tiffany had a point. Given all of the hours I'd be training in the fall to prepare for competition season, and then the Elite qualifier just before Thanksgiving, I'd prob ably miss a lot of school. I'd get a distant, mildly impressed smile from the teacher and a pile of assignments to take home and do at my own pace, and I'd be ignored by the other students just like I was now.

But I couldn't help remembering Dr. Fisher's words to me: *Think about it*. And I couldn't help thinking that right about now was when it would have been nice to have someone to call, some- one who would be excited to hear if we had lunch together or if we had gotten the easy teacher for Biology.

Three

I brought my class schedule to gym to show everyone, even though Noelle and Christina would have had envelopes from the middle school about starting eighth grade, and Britt wouldn't have had any envelope at all. Sometimes I envied her for being homeschooled. She had said it could get kind of lonely, but I felt just as alone in public school.

Noelle and Christina were huddled on a bench in the locker room, their heads together as they spoke in quiet murmurs. Noelle's brown hair was in a bouncy ponytail, and Christina's darker hair was pulled back in an elegant bun, and they both looked totally absorbed in whatever they were discussing.

"Do you guys have classes together?" I asked casually. I hoped they didn't, and then I immediately felt guilty for being so uncharitable.

Noelle slid a piece of paper under her thigh in such a fluid motion I almost wouldn't have known but for the triangle of white that was still visible. "Um, yeah," she said.

I didn't know why she was acting so weird. It was a little awkward that we weren't going to the same school anymore, but that was just the way it was. It wasn't like I didn't see a ton of Noelle, Christina, and Britt at the gym.

"Are you in Advanced English with Ms. King?" I asked.

Christina's eyes darted to Noelle's. "Yes," she said. It sounded more like a question.

I rested one hand on my hip. "Well, look at your schedule," I said impatiently, gesturing toward the piece of paper I knew Noelle was hiding. "What does it say?"

Noelle pulled the paper out and unfolded it in front of her; I didn't have to squint to see the huge, colorful heading at the top.

The letters were printed in bright red and navy blue: USAG. USA Gymnastics.

"What's that about?" I asked. I didn't remember seeing anything in the mail from USAG. If I had, it would've definitely been on my radar, but then again, I'd been distracted by the letter from my school.

"It's about the National team," Christina said apologetically.

Of course. I should've realized—both Noelle and Christina were on the National team now, which meant they'd be getting all kinds of stuff from USAG that Britt and I wouldn't even know about. I made my voice casual, so they would think I didn't care. "What's it say?"

"It's about the stipend," Noelle said. "We need to decide soon if we're going to accept it or not."

I only vaguely knew that gymnasts who were part of the National team were eligible to receive a monthly stipend, to help pay for training. Money or no money—it seemed obvious. Why *wouldn't* you take the extra assistance?

But I didn't have time to ask before Britt burst into the locker room. "What are you guys still doing in here? Practice is about to start."

"We were talking about our school schedules," Christina said quickly. I wondered again why they were being so weird about it. I mean, yeah, they'd made the National team and Britt and I hadn't— Britt because she'd bombed out at the last minute, me because I hadn't even competed in the first place. But there was no need to be so shifty about the whole thing.

I might've called Christina out if Britt hadn't gotten that mischievous smile on her face. It was one way to tell that she had something up her sleeve, although it wasn't the only sign. Britt was up to something anytime she was awake and breathing.

"Did you arrange your first-period P.E.?" she asked. "I did."

I was glad Britt was reminding me. I needed to ask my mom to call the school before I got stuck in a class. "Very funny," I said. "That's the benefit of homeschooling, I guess: nothing to arrange."

"No, I'm being serious," Britt said.

I gave her a doubtful look. Britt joked for fifty-nine minutes of every hour of every day, even if she insisted she was being straight up. Then, when you believed her, ha! She'd have been messing with you the entire time.

"As of a week from Monday," Britt said, "I will be an eighth grade student in the public school system of Travis County, Texas. They're even letting me skip a grade 'cause I'm so darned smart."

"Whoa!" Christina's eyes widened. "That's a big change."

"It'll be cool to have classes with you," Noelle said with a smile.

"So, wait," I said. "You *chose* to go to school with the random weirdos in this city, rather than stay at home doing whatever you want with your grandmother?"

"First of all, I didn't get to do *whatever* I wanted," Britt said. This was a sore point with her. Half the time, she wanted to complain about how her grandmother had such high standards and made her do work that was way harder than anything we had to put up with in public school, and the other half, she wanted to brag about how sweet it was to get to be home all day, making her own schedule, taking field trips wherever she wanted to go.

"Second of all," she continued, "I always got jealous listening to you guys talk about dances and lunches and homework. I think I'm ready to hang out with people other than my grandmother." She smiled ruefully. "And you guys, of course."

As Dr. Fisher had so kindly pointed out, I'd been in the public school system for years and still didn't have any friends outside the gym. Come to think of it, I wasn't particularly close with either of my grandmothers, either. I saw my biological father once a year if I was lucky, saw my stepmonster less often than that; and my stepsiblings might as well have been strangers living in my house for all the attention they paid me.

"For real, though," Britt said, pulling Noelle up off the bench. I saw Noelle shove the folded sheet of paper into her locker, but Britt didn't seem to notice or care. "Time for practice. You know, if Mo has to come in here, she'll give us the death glare."

There had been a time when Britt would've been the last person to be pushing us out the door. When she first came to the gym, she had gotten in trouble for goofing off too much. But that was what I liked about her: she didn't take herself too seriously. Sometimes I got stuck in my own head, and it was nice to have a friend who could pull me out.

We headed out to the floor just in time to start our stretches; I could have done mine in my sleep.

Sometimes at night, if I was having a hard time drifting off, I would do the stretches in bed, bringing my knees up to my nose and back down until I was tired enough to roll over and go to sleep.

Yet another effect of being a gymnast: I couldn't even go to sleep properly. I should have been counting sheep or staring up at a poster of Justin Bieber, but instead I was stretching, always stretching, worrying that if I rested for even a minute I would let all the potential gold medals pass me by.

After a long day at practice, I was heading out of the gym when Britt grabbed me by the sleeve. "Hey," she said. "You got a minute?"

A minute was probably all I had, since my mother would be there to pick me up soon. Britt's mother was notoriously late, so I knew she'd be hanging out for a little while.

"Sure," I said. "What's up?"

I thought maybe she'd ask me why Noelle and Christina had been acting so weird in the locker room, or that maybe she'd noticed how quiet I had been through most of practice. But instead she took a crumpled piece of paper out of her duffel bag, smoothing it out to read to me.

"You have to tell me what I'm in for with these teachers," she said. "I mean, are they hazing me, or what?"

"Hazing?"

She thrust the sheet of paper into my hand impatiently. "Yeah, you know, let's show the home-schooled kid how tough it is on the inside—that sort of thing."

I laughed. I couldn't help it. "It's not prison, Britt."

"I know," she said, "but maybe they're giving me a superhard schedule just to break me. As long as I'm prepared, I won't crack."

I glanced down at her schedule and felt a wave of nostalgia seeing some of my old teachers' names—even the names of the mean ones, and the boring ones—which meant I must have been a real mess. "It does look tough," I admitted.

"I knew it," she said, clenching her fists at her side. "I haven't even started yet and they're messing with me. I figured—"

"Britt." I interrupted her before she could get all worked up. "Did it ever occur to you that they're putting you in hard classes because you're—you know—*smart*? If you're going to blame anyone, it should be your grandmother, for teaching you so much stuff."

"My grandmother's a saint," Britt said, but she was grinning. "Thanks, Jess. I would've asked Noelle and Christina, since they might be in some of my classes, but they were acting all squirrelly about something in the locker room. What's that about?"

Earlier, I had resolved that I would tell Britt what I'd seen. It wasn't that big a secret anyway, since Britt probably knew that gymnasts on the National team got offered a stipend, and she knew that Noelle and Christina were on the National team now. She was good at math; she'd put two and two together.

But for some reason, now I just shrugged. "Who knows?" I said. "It's always crazy when school starts back up. Things will go back to normal."

Britt rolled her eyes. "I hope so, because they were acting weird with a capital *W*. Hey, do you maybe want to get together that first Friday after school? We could compare notes or whatever."

Every now and then Britt showed a small crack in her armor, a tiny sign that, though she might have been fearless when it came to doing a backflip on the balance beam, she had her insecurities just like anyone else. No matter what Dr. Fisher seemed to think about my needing other friends, I figured I had at least one pretty good one already.

"Sure," I said, just as my mom pulled up. "I'll ask if you can spend the night at my house. We can talk about how much we miss summer already."

Four

I'd been to Birchbark High School several times before, a couple of times for my stepsister Tiffany's flag-girl practice, and then once when we'd waited outside it, when my stepbrother Josh had to take the SATs. So all I'd really seen was the parking lot and the football field. I'd never been inside. The open house was my chance to see it up close and personal before school actually started.

A map had come with my schedule, and it showed a main hallway that ran the length of the building, with wings jutting out from that on both the first and second floors. When I glanced again at the packet, I saw that Birchbark High had over a thousand students. I wondered how people avoided getting lost.

It seemed as if there were a thousand people in the cafeteria, even though I knew it would only be the other incoming freshmen and their parents. They had tables set up by last name, and I waited in the G–J line for my name tag and the sheet that would tell me where I needed to go.

My name tag said JESSICA IVY on it in big, bubbly letters, even though practically no one called me Jessica. I glanced around, trying to see if I should stick the tag on my shirt or on some nonconformist place like the bottom of my jean skirt or if I should ball it up and throw it in the trash. I didn't want to seem like a complete dweeb before I even started school. Plus, I knew half of these kids from middle school; why would we need name tags?

"Put your name tag on," my mother said, taking it from me and unpeeling it from its back. Luckily, I intercepted her before she could actually stick it on my chest. In no universe would *that* be cool.

"*Mom,*" I hissed. In the end, I pressed the name tag to my chest anyway. I knew she'd insist on it.

"Now everyone knows who you are," she said,

smiling. "I can't believe my baby's in high school already."

"Please, Mom, not another anecdote about me dancing around the living room or something. Let's just see where we need to go first."

Technically, I was due in my Biology classroom to catch the last five minutes of a meet-and-greet with the teacher, but I still needed to work out the issue of having P.E. at the end of the day, even though my mother had called the school about it several times already. So my mother went to talk to the guidance counselor about switching my schedule, and I decided to check out my American Government class a little early.

The room was on the second floor, and the halls were mostly empty, as everyone had gone to their first-period classrooms. I found the door with the nameplate that read MR. FREEMAN and peered in through the narrow glass window. The teacher was standing at the front of the room; at least, I assumed he was the teacher, given that he was wearing a tie and writing something on the board. He was supertall.

I was still staring through the window, trying to figure out if he looked like his class would be easy or hard, interesting or dull, when he caught sight of me. I slid to the right, hoping that he wouldn't investigate, but then the door opened.

"Hello," he said. "Can I help you?"

"Um, no," I said. "That's okay. I was just . . . looking around."

Up close, he was like that giant in "Jack and the Beanstalk." I'm used to people towering over me, but this teacher was like a basketball player. If I had to sit in class and listen to him lecture, I'd probably have a stiff neck by the end of the day.

"Are you in first-period American Government?" he asked.

This was not how I wanted to meet one of my teachers. "Second-period," I said.

"Well, you're a little early," he said. "But come on in. We can't have you lurking in hallways."

I edged into the room, smiling sheepishly in the direction of the other students and their parents sitting at the desks. I didn't actually make eye contact, because I was hoping that no one would remember this embarrassing interruption once school started. Keeping my eyes lowered, I banged my hip against a desk as I passed. So much for playing it cool.

"Watch it," the girl sitting at the desk said.

I murmured an apology but didn't look up until I was safely seated at one of the back desks. I almost expected Watch-It Girl to have turned around and glared at me, but when I glanced up, she was flicking her long blond hair, her attention back on Mr. Freeman.

"And so that's how grading will work in this class," Mr. Freeman said, finishing a discussion he'd obviously started before my appearance. "Any questions?"

A guy with glasses and light hair that flipped up around his ears raised his hand.

"Yes, Norman?" Mr. Freeman said.

"Do you grade on a curve?" Norman asked. The way he asked the question made it clear he did not approve of that kind of grading. Definitely a suck-up.

Mr. Freeman smiled. "No, Norman, I don't grade on a curve."

Watch-It Girl leaned across the aisle and whispered something to a girl I recognized from last year; her name was Ashley, I remembered. She'd been one of the popular kids, someone I had seen across the lunchroom but never this close up. Her hair was shinier than I remembered it, and so straight it looked like it could have been made of plastic.

"All right, then. Class dismissed," Mr. Freeman said. "If anyone needs help finding their next room, let me know."

As everyone else filed out of the room, including Norman, Watch-It Girl, and Ashley, Mr. Freeman approached my desk. "I can see that you don't need any assistance with that," he said. "Jessica, is it?"

"Jessie," I said, correcting him, wishing again that I wasn't wearing such a stupid name tag.

"Jessie Ivy," he said. "I read about you in the sports section a couple of weeks ago. You're the gymnast, right?"

It was one of the first times I'd ever been recognized in public as a gymnast, almost like I was a celebrity. I felt the heat rising in my cheeks; one of the worst things about being a redhead was the constant threat that your feelings would show all over your face and you'd look like a lobster.

"Yeah," I said. I hoped he wouldn't confuse me with one of the other girls and ask me what medal I'd won.

Other people were starting to trickle into the

room. I glanced around, trying to see if I recognized anyone from middle school. I was relieved that Watch-It Girl and Ashley weren't in my class, or Norman, if he was as smart as he seemed to be.

"It's a tough sport," Mr. Freeman said, sitting on the edge of one of the desks next to me.

In my book, it was the toughest, and it often didn't get the respect it deserved. To be a great gymnast, you had to be strong but flexible, athletic but graceful. I was always happy to hear someone acknowledge that it was more than dancing around and doing somersaults, but I wondered why Mr. Freeman was still talking to me. Shouldn't he have been up at the front of the room, welcoming people coming in?

"High school is difficult, too," Mr. Freeman said. I just looked at him, trying to figure out where he was going with this.

His dark brown eyes were kind as he looked down at me, so much so that his next words almost didn't register. "I'd hate for anyone to think they were getting a free pass on school, just because they had made a choice to focus their energies on something else. This is American Government, a class about democracy. And here, everyone is held to the same standards. Do you understand?"

He tapped my desk, as if to say, *we're done here*, and left me gaping after him. I got his message, loud and clear, but I didn't get why he was saying it to me. All of those times that my mom had called the school about switching my schedule, had she ever said anything that would have led teachers to believe I expected special treatment? It was true that in the past, teachers had often given me extensions on my homework or allowed me to take exams home, to accommodate my busy training schedule, but I had never been called on it before, especially when school hadn't even started yet.

I dimly heard Mr. Freeman giving his welcoming spiel, but I wasn't paying much attention, still too lost in my own thoughts. I didn't even notice my mother slip into the classroom until she had slid into the seat next to mine, leaning in to whisper, "It's all worked out. You'll have P.E. first period, so that you won't miss any morning practice."

I nodded, hoping she would take that as response enough. The last thing I wanted was for Mr. Freeman to assume I thought I could talk through his class, since he obviously already assumed I thought I was entitled to a lot.

"I was able to keep the rest of your schedule the same," my mother said, beaming at me. "This teacher seems nice."

I looked down at my hands, clasped on top of the desk, and wondered how I was going to keep up with the workload Mr. Freeman expected of me, deal with the other pressures of high school, and still stay on top of my gymnastics, all at the same time.

"How was the open house?" my stepdad, Rick, asked that night at dinner. "Did you feel a draft come through?"

I'd been passing the peas to Josh, but stopped to try to decipher Rick's question. "What?"

"It was open, right? So the wind must've gone right through the building."

I should've known it was one of Rick's cheesy jokes.

Still, I made a halfhearted attempt to laugh, just to let him know that I appreciated the effort. Josh rolled his eyes, Tiffany was too busy painting her nails at the dinner table to even notice, and my mother muttered, "Dear Lord," under her breath, as though praying to be saved from Rick's corny humor.

"I can't text my friends during dinner, but Tiffany can have her own salon and spa operating at the table?" Josh said.

My mother drew her eyebrows together to let Josh know she didn't appreciate the tone, but she tapped the table in front of Tiffany's plate. "Put the nail polish away," she said. "It's giving us all a headache."

Now it was Tiffany's turn to roll her eyes, but she obeyed. She was always painting her nails, like there was a rule that they couldn't be the same color for a whole week.

"Is high school much harder than middle school?" I asked. It must've seemed like an abrupt question to the rest of my family, because everyone turned to look at me. But it was something I'd been thinking about ever since my experience with Mr. Freeman earlier that afternoon.

"Is being an Elite gymnast harder than being Level Eight?" Josh asked.

"I don't know," I said. "I'm not technically an Elite gymnast yet."

"Josh," my mother admonished him under her breath.

He waved his fork in a gesture that sent a noodle from his pasta salad flying back onto his plate. "What? I can't keep up with these things. It was a legitimate question. Forgive me for trying to put it in terms I thought she would understand."

I resented the implication that I only spoke in gymnastics lingo, although it was a little bit fair. "Of course it's harder," I said. "It's a higher level. There are bigger skills you need to learn, your technique is graded tougher, and you are competing against the best gymnasts in the world."

Josh jabbed at the air with his fork, although luckily, this time there were no noodles on it. "Well, then. There you go."

Although he came across as a slacker who cared more about hanging out with his friends and playing video games than about school, Josh was really smart. He'd scored only a few hundred points away from perfect on the SATs. So if he said that high school was going to be more of a challenge than middle school, then I should definitely be worried.

As if I hadn't been already.

* * *

At gym, we fell back into a routine, after all the hoopla surrounding the parade and Nationals. Our coaches, Mo and Cheng, made us do the same moves over and over until we got them perfect. For me, it felt like a relief. It had been distracting to have all of that other stuff going on; my mother had taped the brief news segment with my dad, although I hadn't watched it yet. I was anxious just to get back to work.

I landed my double front tuck on the floor a little short, which sent me falling backward on my butt. I was slow to get up, not because I was really hurt, but because this wasn't the first time I'd landed the pass that way, and I was getting sore.

"You're short," Cheng said, waving the next girl on. Noelle flew across the floor, completing her round-off to back handspring to two-and-a-half twist perfectly. It was possibly her simplest pass, but still, it was frustrating to see it coming so easily to her while I was struggling.

I knew I'd been short. He didn't need to tell me that; of course I knew it. My tailbone knew it, and by the time I went to bed that night, I'd have an angry bruise on one butt cheek that would know it, too.

As Christina got set to tumble across the floor, Britt leaned over to whisper, "Duh. Of course you're short."

"Excuse me?" I said, without any thought to controlling the volume of my voice. Cheng glanced over disapprovingly.

Britt didn't have time to respond before it was her turn, and then Cheng was motioning me to follow. I took a deep breath, trying to clear my mind before I took off running, but the only thing swirling around in my head was: *You're short; of course you're short; you're short; of course you're short*. I launched into my front handspring, but I knew I wasn't going to have enough power for the double front, and so I rolled out of the first somersault instead, channeling all of that momentum into a gymnastics move that a three-year-old could do.

Cheng shook his head at me. "Follow through!" he snapped. He was angry, although it was really because he was concerned, since balking on a skill like that could be really dangerous. That was how head and neck injuries happened. I felt shaky even thinking about the possible consequences of such a huge mistake.

I knew I needed to get higher in the air to land the double front properly, but when my feet left the ground, I felt like an anvil. Instead of flying, all I could do was fall.

"Hey," Britt said, jabbing me in the back with her elbow as I took my place at one corner of the floor. "Your *height*."

I really didn't want to get into any more trouble with Cheng, but I couldn't help myself. "What?"

"It was a joke, get it? He said you were short, and I said of *course* you are, because of your height."

When I made a move to turn back around, she jabbed me again.

"Ow!" I said.

"What's wrong?"

Out of the corner of my eye, I saw Noelle land her double twist solidly, and I heard the satisfying thunk of the springboard beneath the floor mat as she planted both her feet. I made a show of rubbing the spot on my back where Britt had elbowed me. "Right now, my only problem is you," I muttered. "We're supposed to be practicing."

"Is it school on Monday?" Britt whispered. But, since Britt's normal volume was decibels above everyone else's, it was more like a loud stage whisper. I shook my head quickly, gesturing for her to be quiet.

"I'm nervous, too," she continued, ignoring me. Cheng was adjusting Christina's position, making his hands into a flat plane to show how her body should look in the air. "But excited. Aren't you excited? I mean, this is our chance."

"Our chance to what?" I asked despite myself. Christina was rubbing her toes in the chalk on the floor, gaining some last-minute traction before she started her tumbling pass.

"Our chance to *reinvent* ourselves," Britt said, her eyes shining. "Nobody knows me at this school—except for Noelle and Christina, of course. And this is your first year of high school. We could talk in British accents or wear fedoras. . . . We could be whoever we wanted to be."

Christina landed her double twist cleanly, with just a small step backward. In a competition, she could have "danced" that step by throwing her hands up in a salute and making it look intentional, and she probably wouldn't even have lost a tenth of a point. Whereas, if I kept landing on my butt or not landing at all, I'd be completely out of the running for any medal.

It was Britt's turn. She gave me a little salute. "Cheerio!" she said, and then she was off, her arms pumping, throwing herself into her round-off to back handspring to whip back to piked full-in. She had a problem opposite from the one I'd been having: she sometimes had too much energy and ended up bounding almost off the floor mat entirely with the force of her landing.

Cheng shouted, "Control!"

It seemed to me like Britt's issues were a lot more fixable than mine. She had all of the power she needed, and all of the confidence; all she had to learn was how to refine it a bit. She'd be brave enough to go into a new school and fake a British accent, but she wouldn't need to do it in the first place. She didn't need to reinvent herself, because she already knew who she was.

Whereas I was starting to feel like I was always coming up short—on my landings, with my friends, with school. If there was anyone who needed reinvention, it was me, but I didn't know if I had what it would take to pull it off.

Cheng nodded for me to go. I stood up on the balls of my feet, preparing to spring into my tumbling pass. This was the moment I always dreaded and looked forward to the most: the moment when I hadn't yet committed to anything, when there were all the possibilities in the world ahead of me. As long as I stayed in this corner, getting ready for my next pass, I hadn't failed yet. I could still tell myself that this time it could be different, that my body could be a feather instead of an anvil, and I just might fly.

The weekend before school started, my mom took me shopping. First, we had to find all of the supplies on the list I'd received in the mail. This year, they wanted me to have a graphing calculator, which cost eighty dollars, and a very specific type of agenda planner, which wasn't easy to find. I thought back to times when my supplies list had consisted of things like Magic Markers and extra tissues for the classroom, but when I pointed that out to my mother, she just waved her hand.

"What was that, elementary school?" she asked. "Although I'll grant you it was cheaper."

Once we were finished with all the supplies, she wanted to take me to the mall for clothes. I tried to convince her that she should just give me some money and I could go with Britt or Christina or Noelle, but she wasn't having it.

"You'll come home with three belts and no pants," she said. "Now, let's hurry, before everything's picked clean."

"It's not like the mall is going out of business," I said.

"Honey, it's the weekend before school starts. Believe me, everyone else has the same idea we do."

As much as I hated to admit it, my mother was right. The department stores were so crowded there were lines for most of the fitting rooms. We were waiting for me to try on some jeans when my mother spotted the lingerie section.

"You don't own a real bra, do you?" she asked, just like that, in the middle of the store. The word *bra* fell off her lips like she was mentioning snow peas or something.

"*Mom!*" I glanced around. I hadn't seen anyone I recognized yet in this mass of people, but I was nervous. They might have been out there, watching this whole exchange and laughing at me, and I wouldn't even have known it. Suddenly, I felt self-conscious, with my petite jeans draped over one arm and a couple of tops in the other. The top that looked like a long-sleeved shirt over a lace-trimmed camisole had *looked* really cool, but now I wasn't so sure. Purple might've been a babyish color for someone in high school.

"I know you have sports bras," she continued, as though she wasn't single-handedly almost causing her daughter's face to implode, "but you're almost fourteen; it's about time you got a real bra, don't you think?"

"I'm fine," I said, hoping she'd drop it.

But she was already heading toward the lingerie section, pulling me along with her, even though it meant we lost our place in line. She started rifling through a rack of flimsy white bras, fingering the lace on one of them as though she were inspecting a fine tapestry.

"You're not supposed to touch them," I said.

She laughed. "Of course you can touch them," she said. "They're just clothes, Jessie." She held up one that had two silky triangles over the chest and a little bow in the middle. Some of the other bras had cups that stuck way out, as though they were just waiting to be filled, but this bra was tiny. Obviously, I knew I didn't have much to fill it with.

I flushed. "I don't need one," I said.

"This is pretty!" she said, looking at the bra as though trying to figure out what my problem was with it. "Do you want to get one in a color? You just have to be careful to wear it with an undershirt, or it could show through."

"I already have what I need," I said. I didn't want to use the phrase *sports bra*, even though I'd used it a million times when I was asking my mother if she'd done my laundry or asking Christina if she'd gotten some new workout clothes for Christmas. But surrounded by all of these lacy things, some with polka dots or black or totally see-through, it didn't seem right to use that term.

"Nonsense," my mom said. "It's your first day of high school. You deserve something that's going to make you feel pretty. What about pink?"

A girl brushed past me, and I instinctively moved in toward the racks to make room. When I glanced up, I saw the girl flicking her long, straight, blond hair over her shoulder, in a gesture I'd seen just the other day. There, standing among the lingerie, was Watch-It Girl, leisurely sliding bras from one side of the rack to the other, stopping occasionally to look at one. I noticed that she wasn't interested in the plain white ones, or the ones with the cute little bows. She had set aside one that was bright turquoise with little white hearts all over it, and another that was black and shiny.

I quickly grabbed my mom's arm. "Okay," I said. "I'll take it."

"Which one?"

"Either. Both. I like them both. Can we just go now?"

"Well, you have to try everything on." She tried to hand me the two bras, and when I didn't take them, she draped them over the jeans. I glanced at Watch-It Girl, but she seemed totally into her shopping and wasn't paying any attention to me. I hoped it would stay that way.

"Fine," I said. "Let's get this over with."

We stood in line for ten minutes; I spent a lot of that time pretending to admire the stitching on a jacket that was hanging on the wall. If I kept my head turned away, and my hair hanging over my face, then maybe Watch-It Girl wouldn't even notice me.

Finally, I made it into the dressing room. I shook my head when my mom offered to come in with me. She used to do that when I was a little kid, but I wasn't a little kid anymore.

"Come out and show me how those jeans fit," she instructed me. "If they're too long, I can go get you the next size down."

"Do I have to?" I asked. I knew I was sounding like a petulant child, but I hated this part. My mother would make me lift my shirt and show her how the jeans fit in the butt, and then she'd jiggle the waistband to make sure they weren't too loose. "I'm almost fourteen, Mom. I think I can handle it."

Playing the age card worked. My mother had that look in her eye that she got sometimes, like she was one second away from pulling out my baby book and oohing and aahing over how many inches my head circumference was when I was born (apparently, I'd had a very large head as a baby).

"Okay," she said. "But do try everything on."

I promised I would, but when I locked the dressing-room door behind me and tried the bras on, all I could do was stare at the three successive versions of myself looking back at me in the full-length mirrors. My red hair was frizzy from all of the humidity outside, with strands standing up all around my head as though I'd been shocked. My lashes, which were the same color as my hair, were too light, I'd always thought. It looked like I barely had any lashes at all. I wished the freckles on my face had had the same problem; instead, these stood out clear as day, little brown specks of imperfection spread across my nose and my cheeks.

I took a deep breath, trying to remind myself of everything I'd talked about with Dr. Fisher. My body image was distorted, so even when I looked at a regular mirror, it was as if I was viewing my body through one of those funhouse mirrors that makes you seem fatter than you really are. But I was normal—better than normal, even. I was an athlete. My body was strong. It could handle everything I demanded of it.

Still, I didn't feel like squirming out of my shorts and T-shirt and standing in my underwear in front of all of those mirrors. I sat down on the small seat in the dressing room and counted to two hundred, figuring that would be enough time for me to have tried everything on.

When I finally emerged, my mother beamed at me. "How'd it all fit?"

"Fine," I lied. And then, to make it more believable, I hung one bra back on the rack. "The elastic on this one pinches."

She took the bra back off the rack, stretching out the elastic band with her fingers, as though testing my claim. "It's just like the other one," she said. "Maybe you just need to adjust the straps. Did you see that you can do that?"

The line for the fitting rooms was thinning out, and I saw Watch-It Girl approaching. *She* didn't have her mom with her; her mom probably thought she was grown-up enough to go shopping all by herself. I tried to snatch the bra back from my mother. "Okay, I'll take it," I said. "Let's just go."

By now, Watch-It Girl was at the front of the line; she looked up. Maybe she won't recognize me, I thought. After all, it wasn't like we knew each other from middle school and she'd only bumped into me briefly at the open house.

But the instant I caught her gaze, I knew that my hopes were in vain. She raked me over with her eyes, and obviously found me wanting. Her hair was straight and glassy and perfect, and she was slim and stylish in her skinny jeans. Meanwhile, I was plagued with hair that was prone to frizz, and my jean shorts made me look like I was going to the playground later.

Watch-It Girl glanced down at the bras in my

hands, and one corner of her mouth lifted. "Adorable," she said. Then she disappeared into one of the dressing rooms.

My mother smiled. "Did you know her?" she asked. "A friend from school?"

"Not really," I muttered. My mother went on, pleased that she'd been vindicated in her choice of undergarments by another teenager's opinion. I just nodded, not wanting to draw her attention to the sarcasm that had clearly been under that compliment, and not wanting to explain that Watch-It Girl was the furthest thing from a friend.

Five

T he first day of school started just
like any other day. I was at the gym early,
doing reps on the uneven bars. One of the
things I'd hated most when I started training to be
an Elite gymnast was waking up when it was still
dark outside, eating an egg-white omelet and fruit
in the car while we made our way to the gym. But
now I kind of liked the sanctity of those hours. It felt
as if no one else was around except us, as if we were
those elves that cobbled shoes for the shoemaker, as
if somehow what we did was secret and important.

High school started earlier than middle school,
so I had to do my final stretches forty-five minutes

before the other girls did, and then my mom picked me up. That was when it started to hit me, and I felt the pit in my stomach growing. Before that, I'd been focusing on my giant hop full, doing it over and over. It was easier to concentrate on swinging all the way around the high bar, stopping in a handstand position, then letting go of the bar, spinning like a top, and then catching it again. *That* was easier than thinking about the day ahead of me.

My mom finally pulled up in front of the school, which seemed eerily quiet, like something out of a zombie movie. I remembered that it was still first period, which meant that everyone would be in their classes.

Normally, students had to check in with the front office if they were late, but because my practice was every day, I didn't have to do that. I wondered if this was the sort of "special treatment" that Mr. Freeman had accused me of wanting, but I tried to shake the thought. I hadn't *asked* for it; it just made sense, given that I was basically doing my P.E. off campus.

The bell rang just as I reached my locker—not that I had anything to put in it or take out of it, but I got a tiny thrill from the clicking sound of the combination lock, which I'd gotten at the open house. All of a sudden, all the doors swung open, and kids starting pouring out of them, talking and laughing and jostling me as they walked past. I knew I was short—I'm *always* one of the shortest kids in my class—but I felt like a piece of lint on the floor compared to everyone else. I hurried to shut my locker and escape into my homeroom.

I had barely sat down when someone poked me in the shoulder. At first, I didn't turn around, in case it was some kind of weird joke where the person taps you on the right shoulder and then, when you swivel your head to the right, you get laughed at because no one is there. But then the poke came again, and so I spun around.

It was that kid who'd been in Mr. Freeman's class before me at the open house—the one who asked if Mr. Freeman graded on a curve. He had a mess of curly blond hair and crooked glasses, which kept sliding down his nose as he talked.

"What?" I said, not bothering to conceal my annoyance.

"Do you have a pen?" he asked.

"You're holding a pencil," I pointed out. He did, in fact, have a pencil in his left hand, with a stubby little eraser that he'd been using to dig into my back. At least he hadn't used the point.

"True story," he said. "But I hate pencils. Pencils are for people who make mistakes. I don't make mistakes."

"But you forgot to bring a pen," I said. "So isn't that a mistake?"

He blinked at me before a wide grin spread across his face, revealing the retainer on his bottom teeth. "You're sharp," he said. "I'm Norman."

At first, I thought he'd said he was *normal*, which I had a definite opinion on. But then I realized he'd just been saying his name, and I was about to give him my name in return when Watch-It Girl and Ashley walked through the door.

Norman must've seen my face fall, because he glanced toward the door and then back at me. "The blond girl is Layla," he said. "If eighth grade is anything to go by, she plans on ruling the school by lunchtime."

I had intended not to respond—I wasn't sure that I wanted people to think I was friends with Norman, with his retainer and his weird pen thing and his dislike of grading on a curve. But I couldn't help sighing and saying, "She's so pretty."

"Just ask her," Norman said, and when I only looked at him in reply, he added, "Because she'd agree with you. About being pretty. Because she's stuck-up."

"I got it," I said, sinking down further in my seat and hoping she wouldn't see me.

"Do you want the bio?" he asked, pausing only a second before rattling it off. "She's *MTV Cribs* rich, takes her two closest friends to her daddy's penthouse suite on Central Park every summer, and was unanimously appointed captain of the JV cheer squad before the first practice. She's a monster."

And she had seen—and mocked—the tiny precious bow on my first "real" bra. I wanted to die.

Watch-It Girl—Layla— was giggling in the corner with Ashley, and a paranoid part of me couldn't help thinking it was about me. I just didn't understand why they would hate me on the first day. Ashley had gone to my middle school, but our paths had never crossed, and Layla had bumped into me twice. That was it.

But it was hard to convince myself that it was all in my head when Layla started walking toward me. I turned around in my seat and willed Norman to stop talking.

In the two minutes I had known him, however, Norman didn't seem like the type to do anything someone else wanted him to do.

"Uh-oh," he said. "Incoming."

If Layla heard him, she ignored him. "Are you Jessie Ivy?" she asked.

They *had* been talking about me. And Ashley must've told Layla something—but what? I had been in high school for less than ten minutes, and already I was an outcast. A pariah. At least in eighth grade I'd been invisible. This was worse.

"Um, yes?" I said.

She rolled her eyes. "Are you not sure?"

"Yes," I said. "I mean, yes, I'm sure. I'm Jessie Ivy." I didn't voice my biggest question, which was *Why do you want to know?*

"Ashley says that you're a gymnast," she said.

"Yes," I said, making an effort to sound more authoritative, even though I wished I knew where she was going with this. If she was about to make fun of me for being a gymnast, I thought I'd better downplay it.

For a few moments she just looked at me, as though deciding something. "Can you do a back handspring?"

"Yes."

"Back tuck?"

"Yes."

"Front tuck?"

"Yes."

"Full twist?"

Norman was watching the entire conversation like it was a tennis match. I could tell by the way that Layla twisted her mouth that she thought she had me on this one. I said with a certain relish, "Yes, I can do a full twist."

The only acknowledgment of this statement was a brief raising of Layla's eyebrows. "Cheer tryouts are this Friday at six o'clock," she said. "See you there."

And just like that, she walked away, leaving Norman looking at me as though I was one of those reptiles in the nocturnal exhibit at the zoo. Except that Norman seemed like someone who'd have found those creatures fascinating, and that was how he was staring at me now, as though he'd read on the placard that I had a regenerated tail and he was trying to get a glimpse of it.

"Jessie Ivy," he said. "This is going to be interesting."

* * *

At practice that afternoon, Mo had to tell us multiple times to stop talking and get back to work. It seemed like everyone was buzzing about school. *Can you believe we have to read that whole book? Marissa got so tan over the summer; she looks like an Oompa-Loompa. Social Science is such a joke—he's just going to show us movies all the time.*

I was mostly quiet, laughing at the appropriate moments but lost in my own thoughts. I didn't get some of the other girls' references, and the ones I did get made me nostalgic. I thought about sharing my story of the cheerleading tryouts and the run-in with Layla, but something made me keep it to myself.

"Girls!" Mo yelled at us for the tenth time, and Britt made a show of keeping a straight face, although she couldn't stop a giggle from leaking through. Mo shook her head slightly, but I could tell that she wasn't really mad. It was always like this when we started school again or came back from vacations.

With half an hour of practice still left, Mo told us to stop early, do our last stretches, get changed in the locker room, and then meet her back out on the floor. We all looked at each other with the same thought reflected in our eyes: we hoped we weren't in some kind of trouble.

"Mo and Cheng are moving back to China, and we'll have to coach ourselves," Britt predicted, pulling a long-sleeved shirt on over her leotard. "Imagine a training montage of us on the playground, doing giant swings on the jungle gym and vaulting over those springy animal things."

It occurred to me that Norman and Britt might really get along.

"They wouldn't move back to China," Noelle said. "Especially not now, with . . ." She trailed off, but I knew what she was about to say. Not now, with the international event only a few months away. I wondered how long it was going to be before she and Christina stopped feeling so weird about mentioning it in front of Britt and me.

"Springy animal things?" Christina repeated, obviously hung up on Britt's comment. "What are you talking about?"

"They're shaped like tigers, or frogs or whatever," Britt said. "And you ride them like a rocking horse, but they're on springs. Obviously, you couldn't really vault over them. You'd fly across the playground."

"What do you think Mo's talk could be about?" Noelle asked me, while Christina and Britt moved on to discussing why Britt was throwing clothes over her sweaty leotard instead of just changing into a new outfit.

Britt pointed out that this was what she *always* did, and besides, who had the time to change completely? Christina said that *she* made the time, and anyway, if Britt was going to wait around while everyone else changed, why not just do the same?

I realized Noelle was still waiting for an answer. "I don't know," I said, rather than voice my true fear, which was that the meeting would be about me, and about how maybe I didn't belong on the Elite team if I was doomed never to qualify as an Elite gymnast.

"Well, I guess we're about to find out," Britt said, having sprayed some kind of body mist all over herself. She'd been protesting against Christina's allegations that she would stink up the place if she didn't change; now she smelled strongly of lemons and coconut. And a little bit of sweat.

We left the locker room and sat cross-legged on the blue carpet of the floor mat, waiting patiently for Mo to address us. She was over by the front desk talking to a woman we'd never seen before. To our surprise, Mo pulled over two folding chairs, and the two women sat down in front of us. The woman we didn't know was wearing a polo shirt with the USAG logo on it, which immediately made us all straighten our backs and sit taller. USA Gymnastics was the leading organization in the country for our sport, the one that made all the decisions about what the various skills were going to be worth, what you'd need to do to qualify for the next level, even who would make the Olympic teams.

Our parents were there, too, which meant that it had to be serious. Christina's mom was in the gym all the time anyway, but Britt's mom had taken time off from her busy day-care job, and Noelle's dad had shown up, since her mother was probably at home with Noelle's twin brothers. I used to think that his big mustache made him look a little scary, until I got to know him a bit better. It turned out that he was really nice, but very quiet.

My mom was there, too, and I waved at her. There wasn't time to do anything else, since Mo was already addressing our group.

"Two of you make National team," Mo said, and my heart sank. It was just as I'd thought: she would congratulate Noelle and Christina, tell Britt she should keep at it, and then tell me that, since technically I wasn't an Elite gymnast, perhaps I should train with the lower-level girls. It was like one of those children's activity books. *Which one of these does not belong?*

"There is much decision that go along with making National team," Mo continued. "I have here a representative from USAG, who can tell you about it. Ms. Carroll?"

The woman seated next to Mo started to say, "Thank you. Girls, I wanted—" But before she could finish, Britt raised her hand. "Yes, Brittany?"

Britt seemed taken aback that Ms. Carroll knew her name. "Just Britt," she said. "And I didn't make the National team. So do I still need to be here?"

Ms. Carroll glanced at Mo.

"Everyone need to listen," Mo said, her lips tightening. We all knew that face; it meant, *stop asking questions and just do as I say.* I saw it a lot when Mo had me practice my split leaps with weights around my ankles, over and over until my muscles burned. If I asked her when I could stop, she'd get that look, and that was my cue to keep leaping.

"Britt—" Ms. Carroll glanced at me and smiled. "—*And* Jessie. You're both very talented. I have no doubt you'll join our National team in the next couple of years. So, yes, I think it would benefit you to listen, as well.

"When you're one of the top athletes in the country, you join that country's team. At that point, you're no longer competing just for yourself, but representing America in international competitions. Noelle, Christina, I know you will both have the opportunity to attend a training camp that will select this year's team for international events. As you're both aware, the next invitational coming up is called USA vs. the World, where some of our finest gymnasts will compete against top gymnasts from Russia, Romania, and China."

Noelle and Christina glanced at each other, unconcealed excitement on their faces. I picked at one of the blue fibers in the carpet.

"One of the benefits of being on the National gymnastics team is that USAG offers a monthly stipend to its athletes, to help offset the costs of training. This money goes directly to your parents, and it's up to them how it is allocated—whether on competition fees, new equipment, or leotards, or your weekly fees to Texas Twisters."

I hoped my mother wasn't angry with me for

not doing better so I could earn this money, too. I was already beginning to feel bad enough about it myself.

"You can choose to decline this money, and if you do, you can always choose to accept it at a later date. It's yours as long as you're on the National team."

"Wait, why would anyone turn it down?" Britt blurted out, then raised her hand. "Sorry. But I'd be cashing that check faster than you could say Nadia Comaneci."

Noelle tugged on the end of her ponytail, something I knew she did when she was thinking about something. "If you take it, you can't compete in college," she said. Then she flushed. "Scott told me about it. He had to say no to the money so that he could get his scholarship."

Scott was an older gymnast whom Noelle had had the biggest crush on for forever. But ever since the summer, she'd been kind of flirting with a guy from school, although she had vowed not to date him until she won an Olympic gold medal. Still, Scott had come back to the gym a couple of times, and he and Noelle were still friendly.

"That's right," Ms. Carroll said. "The NCAA

doesn't allow its athletes to accept money for their sport, and that includes this stipend. So if you wanted to compete at the college level, you'd have to retain your amateur status."

My stepdad, Rick, watched a lot of sports programs, and I remembered hearing about this kind of thing before. Football players got in trouble for living in houses that other people had paid for and for getting free dinners and cars. But it seemed unfair to apply this rule to gymnastics, since football was a sport that guys could play in high school for free, while gymnastics was an expensive sport that wasn't offered at most schools. At least, not in the Austin area.

"I'll be seventeen at the next Olympics," Britt said. "And after I win my gold medal, I'm going to do one of those big tours, where you get to wear costumes and do routines to songs with words in them. So I'm not really worried about college, anyway."

Ms. Carroll cocked her head, as though considering what Britt had said. I noticed that beneath her smooth dark hair were dangling earrings shaped like ballet shoes. "That's certainly a factor," she said. "If you decide to compete in professional exhibitions, you'd lose your eligibility anyway, so you might as well accept the stipend. But keep in mind that, although the Olympics may be your goal, only five girls in the whole country get to be part of that team, and you could be injured, or be a bars specialist when they need a beam worker, or just have a bad day. So it could be smart to keep your options open."

Ms. Carroll went on to discuss more hypotheticals, and Christina's mother interrupted with several questions, but I tuned it all out. After all, what was the point? My chances of making the Olympic team seemed pretty slim; I wondered if any colleges would even want me.

Ms. Carroll took one final question from Mrs. Flores and then finished her talk, and she was packing some papers into her briefcase when I approached her. The other girls had moved away and were busy chattering about everything they'd just learned. Even Britt's eyes were shiny with anticipation. *She'd* almost definitely make the team next year.

"Thank you," I said to Ms. Carroll, because I thought it was the polite thing to do. And then, on a whim, I added, "I like your earrings."

She touched her fingers to one sparkling slipper, as though reminding herself which ones she had on. "Well, thank you," she said.

"Were you a ballerina?"

"Ballerina, cheerleader, rhythmic gymnast, you name it," she said. "I was never great at one thing, but I was fairly good at lots of things to make up for it." She laughed. "Did you have any other questions?"

I wasn't sure if I was even fairly good at the one thing I'd chosen to do with my life. But that was a question that she couldn't answer. "No," I said. "No more questions."

Six

Usually on Friday afternoons when we got out of practice, everyone went to get frozen yogurt—the four of us, Mo, and our parents. Britt's mom tried to make it when she could, but Friday evenings were busy for her at the day care, and Britt's dad was some big-time chef who'd had a small bit on a cooking show once, and so he was always working at peak dining hours. My parents worked, too, and so they often couldn't come, and Noelle's family ran their own store. Sometimes Noelle's mom would bring the four-year-old twins and have yogurt with us, but usually it was just Christina's mom,

Mrs. Flores, who never missed a gymnastics function.

I'd meant to say something all through practice about missing out on frozen yogurt that afternoon, but I didn't know how to bring it up. So instead, I waited until my mother arrived at the gym for me.

"How wonderful that your mother could make it," Mrs. Flores said as she saw her walking toward us. My mom was coming from her job as an office manager, which meant that she was wearing her standard button-down shirt, with the sleeves rolled up, and a pair of black pants. Mrs. Flores, on the other hand, always wore something striking and different, like the black-and-white print dress she had on today. I saw her gaze sweep over my mom and wondered what she thought.

"Oh," I said. "Actually . . ."

My mother came up and put her arm around me, leaning down to give me a kiss.

"Hi, Mrs. Flores," she said, smiling at Christina's mom. "Hello, girls. Jess, are you ready to go?"

"Should I ride with you?" Britt asked us. "I have my stuff in my bag."

I'd forgotten all about Britt spending the night.

With everything going on—the first week of school, grueling workouts at gym, and Ms. Carroll's talk—we hadn't had much time to discuss it.

My mom looked puzzled; I jumped in to clarify the situation. "Actually, I have something else I have to do today," I said. "So I can't go this time."

Everyone stopped and looked at me. This was our weekly team-building time, and Mo treated it almost like an extension of our practice. People had missed before, but usually only because a relative was in town, or someone was sick, or a big competition kept all of us from being able to go.

Noelle's eyes turned sympathetic. "We understand," she said. "That's okay."

I realized that she must have thought that the other commitment was related to my therapy, and so she wasn't going to press the issue. I would've considered letting it go at that, except that Christina asked outright, "What is it?"

Before I could think about how to answer that question, my mom squeezed my shoulder. "Jessie's trying out for the cheerleading squad," she said. "We have to get going if we're going to make it."

Everyone was just staring at me; I gave them all a weak smile. "Tell Mo I'm really sorry," I said. Mo had already left to run an errand and was going to meet everyone later, and although I was relieved not to have to talk to her about this face to face, I was dreading her reaction.

"So . . . are we not hanging out tonight?" Britt asked, and she had that look on her face, the one that said that she wasn't mad yet, but she was hurt, and that could almost be worse.

"We can," I said quickly, hoping to salvage something from the situation. "Mom, I'm sorry, but I forgot to ask. Can Britt come over tonight?"

My mother agreed. Mrs. Flores offered to drop Britt at my house, since it was on her way home from the yogurt place, and Britt looked slightly mollified.

"We'll talk tonight," I said.

"We'd better," she replied. "Seems like there's a lot of catching up to do."

Britt's words seemed ominous, but I didn't have time to dwell on them as I left the gym, the knots in my stomach tightening with every step. For as long as I could remember, I had considered myself a gymnast. Now, I was about to see if I could be a cheerleader as well.

* * *

"So nice of you to join us," Layla drawled when I was finally crossing the wide wooden floor of Birchbark High's basketball court. Next to her, a girl snickered, but Ashley gave me a smile, which surprised me. Had I missed something? Had Ashley known who I was last year and thought that I was someone worth smiling at?

"Sorry," I said. "I have gym practice pretty late, so this was the earliest I could get here."

Layla looked intrigued in spite of herself. "How many days a week do you practice?"

"Every day but Sunday," I said.

She tapped her pencil on the clipboard in front of her. "So, you must be pretty good," she said. "Show us that full twist."

I was a little taken aback at being asked to do something right on the spot, with no mats and no opportunity to stretch. Normally, I was careful about that kind of thing. But I wanted to impress Layla and I didn't want to make any excuses. I took a deep breath and launched myself into a round-off full twist.

My knees had been bent—a detail that Cheng would've surely called me on, if he were there. Or at least he would've given me that *look*, the one that

80

said he was watching and knew I'd made a mistake. But the corners of Layla's mouth turned down, and she nodded. "Not bad," she said.

In the corner, I noticed a woman who must have been the cheerleading coach; she was writing something on the clipboard in front of her. I hoped it was good.

"Let's hear a cheer," the girl next to Layla said. Her voice was less than friendly, and I remembered that she was the one who'd laughed at me earlier, when I mentioned gymnastics. She was in my English class—I thought her name was Stephenie.

"I don't think I know any," I said.

"You must know *one*," she said snidely, as though that knowledge was something that everyone was born with. Two eyes, a nose, a mouth, and the ability to spit out at least one cheer on demand.

I tried to think back to cheers I'd heard Tiffany do. She was a flag girl now, but she'd been a cheerleader for youth football, and it seemed like I might've heard one of her old cheers around the house.

"Oh!" I said. "I have one."

The three girls looked at me, waiting.

"Ready? Okay!" I said, clasping my hands in

front of my chest. That seemed like a safe way to start.

"Florida oranges, Texas cactus," I chanted. I wasn't sure what to do with my hands, so I made a circle for the word *oranges* and held my arms up like a cactus for the second part.

"We think your team needs a little practice!" That part was a little easier, since I could point at my chest for *we,* out at them for *your,* and then do a little shimmy on the word *practice.* As if they were practicing dancing? I didn't know, but I knew cheerleading meant more than just standing in one place, so I was trying to act it out.

"Put 'em in a high chair, feed 'em with a spoon..." I squatted, as though sitting in a high chair, and mimed eating with a spoon. But then I hesitated, unable to remember the next line.

"Something something something something," I said weakly, doing a disco dance to the beat of each word. I decided to end with a flourish, to make up for my mess-up. I kicked one leg high in the air, my knee almost touching my nose, and said, *"And kick 'em to the moon!"*

For effect, I did a straddle leap and landed with my arms in the air, shouting, *"Go, team!"* waving my fingers like I saw cheerleaders do sometimes on TV.

For a second, all I could hear was the sound of my own breathing, as the three girls stared back at me. And then, so quiet I almost didn't hear it, there was a small snort from Stephenie as she hid her mouth behind her hand.

"We'll be in touch," Layla said.

Britt was waiting for me when I got home. I could see all of the questions in her eyes.

"Come on," I said. "Let's go to my room."

"So," she said once she'd cleared herself a spot on my bed. To my mother's never-ending chagrin, my room always looked like it had just been hit by a hurricane. "Let's start with the big stuff. Cheerleading?"

I shrugged one shoulder awkwardly. "It seemed like something fun to try. It's not that far off from gymnastics, you know."

"Except that you wear kicky little skirts and shout stupid rhymes," Britt said. "And they do those split leaps that just look silly."

"They're called hurkeys," I said, because I'd watched a couple of videos on YouTube to prepare for the tryouts. "And it doesn't matter, because I don't think I made the team."

Another friend might've asked what had happened, but Britt just waved her hand. "Good riddance," she said. "Like you have time for cheerleading, anyway."

I didn't know if I was relieved or offended by her dismissal. "Yeah, I guess."

"So, let's get to the important stuff," Britt said. "Namely, that you've been holding out on me. How is it that you never told me how good school food is?"

Most people were still uncomfortable talking to me about food or weight; I was glad that Britt was able to be so casual about it. I decided that I didn't need her to back me up on the cheerleading thing; she was probably right. It had been a dumb idea. I had more than enough going on with gymnastics, and I would never make the National team or even the Elite squad if I didn't devote myself to it completely.

After I let Britt know that she was *crazy* for thinking that the school's bland grilled chicken was anything but gross and rubbery, we moved on to talk about other school things. She seemed interested in

Norman, just as I thought she'd be, although she refused to be impressed by the fact that he'd used the word *unanimous*. She said that if everyone voted for one person, then there was no other word to use, so it wasn't that *formidable*, a word that I thought she might be using incorrectly, though I wasn't sure.

At one point, Britt reached under her back to retrieve something she'd been lying on. "What's this?" she asked, pulling out a card, but before I could grab it from her, she opened it.

"*Birthdays are special, it is true, birthdays are special, and so are you,*" she read; but she didn't read the signature, for which I was grateful. I knew what it said by heart: *Happy Birthday, Tiger! Love, Dad.*

"Which birthday was this from?" she asked.

"This one," I muttered.

I could see Britt's thoughts written on her face, but she didn't voice the question of why the card was so obviously designed for a seven-year-old. Instead, she just said, "I thought it was in a few weeks."

"It is," I said, reaching for the card. Britt gave it up without a fight, and I shoved it into a desk drawer. I'd only had it in my bed because . . . well, because sometimes I liked to lie there and look at it, and wonder if there was a reason he'd picked it for me. "He sent it early, that's all."

"Cool," she said.

"It's better than sending it late," I pointed out.

"True," she said. "That's cool."

We were silent for a moment as I ran my finger along the back of my desk chair and Britt stared at the ceiling. "He's going to take me out to dinner for my birthday," I said. "Somewhere fancy. My mom said I might need to get a new dress."

"Don't let it be anywhere French," Britt said. "They make you eat snails and frog legs and stuff. Go to an Italian place. Spaghetti is good no matter how much weird stuff they put into it."

Britt had gone to New York City once with her grandmother for a field trip, where they went to art museums and explored historical places. She was probably the most cultured person I knew, so I appreciated the advice.

Mostly, I appreciated her not saying what I knew she was thinking: that my dad had promised to take me camping earlier this summer, and hadn't. Or that he'd shown up for the parade and then left fifteen minutes later. I knew his track record wasn't great, but he was still my dad.

Suddenly, there was a grinding noise that I couldn't place, until I remembered my cell phone on the desk. My mom had asked me to use it only in emergencies, and I didn't talk to many people on the phone anyway, so I often forgot I even had one. Britt's mom wouldn't let her have one at all, so she couldn't understand how I didn't spend every waking minute using mine.

"Sorry," I said, checking the screen. It said I had a text message from a number I didn't recognize.

I frowned as I clicked on the little envelope. *UR IN*, it read.

"What is it?" Britt asked.

"I don't know," I said. The number had an Austin area code, so it was definitely local. *WHO IS THIS?* I texted back.

A nanosecond later, my phone vibrated again. *LAYLA*, it said, and even through the screen I got the feeling she was frustrated that I'd needed to ask. *U GAVE UR # ON YOUR APP? NEWAYZ, PRCTICE ON MON AT 4. C U THERE.*

"Who is it?" Britt asked.

"No one," I said, but I had a hard time hiding my smile. "It's nothing."

Seven

I 'd looked up a glossary of cheerleading terms online and watched more
YouTube videos in preparation for my first
cheerleading practice, hoping that it would make
me fit in a little better with the other girls. I'd seen
a couple of competitions on television—there were
only a few gymnastics competitions televised each
year, so I had to take what I could get, which meant
I DVR'd anything remotely acrobatic.

At cheer practice, I mostly tumbled. Our coach,
who happened to be the psychology teacher, Ms.
Hinnen, called out positions to each of the girls, and
they would get into pyramid formations. Some girls

formed the bases, meaning that they held the other girls up, and we had three "flyers": Layla, Ashley, and Stephenie. I asked the coach if I was going to be a flyer or a base, and she pointed to a spot on the football field a few yards away.

"Wait there for your cue," she said. "When the flyers get lifted up, but before the basket toss, you tumble a path in front of them. Got it?"

Not really. "What do you want me to do?"

"Tumble in front of them," she repeated impatiently. "Stephenie! Get that leg up!"

I had meant specifically what moves she wanted me to do—front tumbling, back tumbling, cartwheels. But I didn't want to bother her again, so I stood on the mark she'd indicated and waited for the three girls to be lifted into the air. Once their arms were raised to the sky, preparing for the basket toss, I started flipping, performing a round-off into back handspring after back handspring after back handspring, and ending with a back tuck.

"Good," Ms. Hinnen said, but she wasn't looking at me. "Again."

"What about the full twist?" Layla asked.

"You're not ready for a full-twisting basket toss," Ms. Hinnen said shortly, and Layla flushed.

"Not me," she said, "Jessie." She turned to me, blowing her bangs out of her eyes with one puff. "I thought you were doing a full twist!"

"Oh," I said. That had been exactly the kind of information I was looking for from Ms. Hinnen— the exact skills I was supposed to be doing. "I mean, I can . . ."

I really didn't want to. Doing a full twist on the floor, which was springy and padded, was no problem at all. That skill was hardly even worth anything in gymnastics, it was so easy. But doing it over and over on grass seemed like a recipe for disaster.

"Okay, Jessie," Ms. Hinnen said. "Put the full twist in there at the end. Again!"

I took my place and waited for my cue, and at the right moment, I took off into the same tumbling pass, with back handsprings to travel the length of the field in front of the other cheerleaders, and then a tucked full twist to finish.

We took a break to drink some water, and Layla came up to me, breathing hard. "You tucked it," she said.

It took me a second to catch up with her. "Oh," I said. "Yeah."

"At tryouts you laid it out," she said, swigging an entire paper cup's worth of water in a single gulp.

Doing the twist with a stretched-out body was a little harder and required a stronger push-off from the back handspring to get the right air. Otherwise, you risked not being able to make it all the way around, and landing on the grass.

"Do you think I could ever be a flyer?" I asked tentatively. I could do these tumbling passes in my sleep, but doing a full-twisting basket toss seemed like a challenge. None of these girls could do it yet, but I thought with my intense gymnastics training, I might be able to get it.

"We kind of decided who got to be what during summer practices," she said. She had taken her cell phone out of her purse and was busy texting. "Sorry."

I nodded, even though I knew she wasn't looking at me. "No problem," I said. "I just want to help the team."

She glanced up at me, pushing her bangs out of her eyes. Her nails were painted blue, one of Birchbark High's school colors. I hardly ever painted my nails a color, because it wasn't allowed at competitions, and so we all got into the habit of using clear polish only. Tiffany always said it was the stupidest rule she'd ever heard.

"Your full twist is awesome," she said. "That's what this team needs. Seriously, when Ashley told me you were a gymnast, I was, like, so excited."

"Really?" I said. I winced at the squeak in my voice.

"Totally," she said. "If you could just lay it out, it could be amazing. Actually, what about a double twist? Is that something you could do?"

I'd never done a double twist on anything other than a mat or into anything but a foam pit, but I supposed it was possible. "If I tucked it," I said, "it might be doable."

Out of the corner of my eye, I noticed Stephenie and Ashley watching us as Layla smiled at me. "Maybe you could come to my house sometime," she said. "We could work on it together."

It looked like Stephenie was frowning, but at that moment, I didn't want to dwell on it. I was pretty sure that this was exactly what Dr. Fisher had meant when she'd talked about my making friends outside of school. I'd just been invited over to someone's house—and not just anyone's, but Layla's—one of the most popular girls in school.

"Yeah," I said. "Definitely."

I was dying to talk to Britt about Layla and the cheerleading practice, but it still felt awkward, so I left it alone. I wished I could've avoided the discussion with Mo, too, but coaches were a lot harder to dodge than best friends.

"Jessie?" she said when I arrived for practice. "I see you in my office."

It wasn't a question, so I followed her into her office. The last time I'd been in that room, it had been when Mo had had to give my mom the speech about how she wanted to make sure that all Texas Twisters athletes were healthy, and that she had reason to be concerned about me. It made me want to shrink to two inches high just remembering it. Logically, I knew it had all been for the best, but it still made me cringe to think about it.

Now, I couldn't shake the feeling that this was going to be another one of those conversations. I took my seat across from Mo's desk and watched her close the door.

"You miss team time," she said.

I was quiet, not sure if I should apologize or act like it was no big deal. But it was impossible to outlast Mo's silences, so I ended up doing both.

"Sorry," I said. "It was this school thing. . . . It was kind of last-minute."

"So you join cheerleading squad," she said, but again it wasn't a question.

"It's almost like extra workout time," I said. "I may have to miss an hour or so a week of practice, but I'm mostly tumbling, so it's similar to the reps we do on floor. . . ."

I trailed off, intimidated by Mo's level gaze. It was hard to tell what she was thinking, or how much trouble I was in. When she spoke, her voice wasn't angry, but it was firm.

"You can't do both," she said.

I started to protest, but Mo held up her hand.

"I not saying you have to pick gymnastics," she said. "But you are training to be Elite gymnast. That is not hobby. Cheerleading is hobby."

So I wasn't allowed to have interests outside the gym? I knew better than to voice this thought, but it turned out that I didn't need to. Among Mo's other powers, she could apparently read minds.

"You want to have fun outside of gym," she said, "you read. You watch movie. You knit."

Knit?

"You don't put more stress on body," she continued. "You put enough stress here. At home, your body needs to rest. Yes?"

Now, it was almost like I could read *her* mind. I could tell, even though she didn't say it, that she was thinking about the same conversation I'd been remembering when I went in there. She hadn't felt like I was ready to compete in the Elite qualifier then, and she didn't think I could take on cheerleading now.

"I'd like to try it," I said. Mo raised her eyebrows slightly, but nobody could have been more astonished than I was at the words coming out of my own mouth. "If I can do it without it interfering with my training here, I'd really like to keep doing it."

"The next Elite qualifier is in November," Mo said. "Will that be problem?"

Only a week ago, I'd sat in Mr. Freeman's class, and he'd been handing out his syllabus. When I saw that his midterm was right around Halloween, I'd blanched for a second, and he'd stopped and asked,

"Is there a problem?" I had said there wasn't then, and I said there wasn't now.

Mo rose, and so I stood up also, but before I could leave, she said, "Did you like Ms. Carroll's talk?"

"Yes," I said, even though I hadn't understood why I'd had to listen to it. I wasn't the one being offered money by USAG for gymnastics. "Very much."

"Good." She nodded. "I hope it make you think about long-term, not just short-term. Yes?"

"Yes," I said, although I still didn't see what Ms. Carroll had to do with me. At this point, I only wanted to get out of the office and onto the vault, where I could lose myself in timers, running toward the vaulting table and attacking it over and over, doing simple flips that allowed me to get the feel of the springboard for takeoff and the mat underneath my feet on the landing.

More and more, I was learning to appreciate the repetitive, mindless aspects of gymnastics, the things that I felt like I was actually good at. Let Britt, with her fearlessness, take the full twists on the balance beam. Let Christina, with her grace, take the ring leaps on the floor. And let Noelle, with her precision, take the release skills on the uneven bars. I'd be the one who did four back handsprings in a row into a full twist, again and again and again.

Eight

Dr. Fisher's appointment before mine ran a little over, so I had to stay in the waiting room longer than usual. When she finally opened the door to let me in, she offered me something to drink.

"I have water, juice, Coke . . ." she said, and it occurred to me that even now she was giving me a statement, instead of a question.

"Water," I said, although I wasn't that thirsty.

She poured some from a pitcher into a glass with no ice, and I took my seat on her leather sofa.

"Last week you were telling me about that

girl—" She consulted her notes. It occurred to me how weird Layla would think I was if she knew I talked about her like this, in this room filled with books and plants, where my therapist wrote her name down on a yellow pad as part of my case file. "—Layla. She'd invited you to try out for the cheer-leading squad."

For once, I was eager to talk about something, hoping that Dr. Fisher, at least, would be on my side. She was the one who'd wanted me to do more outside the gym, after all. So I told her everything: about how I had made the squad, even after I thought I'd embarrassed myself with my cheer, and about how Layla had complimented me in practice and wanted to hang out, and about how Mo seemed to think that I couldn't do both.

"And you think you can," Dr. Fisher said in that annoying way she had, where it was impossible to tell if she was agreeing with me or doubting me.

"I think I should be able to *try*," I said. "Cheer-leading only takes up a couple hours a week, and it's mostly tumbling, so it's like I'm practicing for gym, anyway." I realized I was repeating the same argument I'd given Mo, and the one I'd told myself over and over again.

"Plus," I said, warming to my subject, "a cheerleading squad is a real team. Texas Twisters isn't a real team."

I hadn't fully put that into words before, but now that I did, something about it resonated within me. At Texas Twisters, my teammates were my direct competitors—they'd made the Elite team when I hadn't, and if we ever competed at Elite meets together, they could end up the ones who would knock me out of contention for a medal. As a gymnast, you could represent your country or your gym, but when you got up there on that balance beam, it was just you.

"Like, a cheerleading squad has bases and flyers," I explained. "Without the bases, who would hold up the flyers and toss them in the air? And without the flyers, what would the bases do?"

"And you are a . . ." Dr. Fisher paused, waiting for me to fill in the blank.

I took a sip of my water, which was lukewarm and tasted slightly of lemon. "I'm their tumbling expert," I said proudly. "No one else can do all the stuff that I can, so it adds another layer to all their routines."

Dr. Fisher nodded, but she looked like she was

thinking something else. One of the problems with therapy was that she got to ask all the questions—or make statements for me to elaborate on, as the case might be. But I was left to wonder what she made of everything I told her, because she didn't always say, even when she was writing stuff down in her notebook.

"You wanted me to get friends outside of the gym," I said accusingly. "You were the one who said that."

"I suggested it might benefit you," Dr. Fisher clarified. "Remember, Jessie, that in this room it's not about what I want or what anyone else wants; it's about *you*."

That sounded like her way of weaseling out of it. She'd told me I should have friends with other interests, and now that I'd made a few—and not just any friends, but girls who were popular and wore makeup and straightened their hair—she was hedging. I didn't get it.

"Nothing I've been doing until now has gotten me anywhere," I pointed out. "I didn't make the National team. . . . I didn't even compete. I'm not even an Elite yet, technically."

She consulted her notes, flipping back to a

previous page. "I thought you said you would be able to qualify soon," she said.

I stared at my glass of water. The sun's rays were refracted through the glass and made a couple of light stripes on the wooden table. I'd put a coaster under my drink, even though it wasn't sweating, because this seemed like the kind of place where you always used coasters.

"The next qualifier is coming up in a couple of months," I said. "And I'm still going to compete. I'm just going to be cheering at the same time. Why is that so hard to get?"

I would've never talked to my mother or Mo in that tone, but Dr. Fisher was different. That was one thing I kind of liked about therapy: I could say anything I wanted to, and Dr. Fisher didn't yell at me.

Instead, she treated my question seriously. "I think it's hard for people to understand, because it's unlike you," she said. "For years you've been working toward your goal of being a gymnast, and now you're making a choice that could be viewed as going against that goal."

"I'm *reinventing* myself," I said, slapping the arm of the couch. My open palm against the leather made a louder sound than I had expected, and I closed my hand into a fist. "I thought that's what you wanted." Noticing the expression on Dr. Fisher's face, I corrected myself. "Okay, not what you wanted, but what you thought would be good for me."

Dr. Fisher regarded me from behind her glasses. They were funkier than what I thought a therapist would pick out, with red frames and three tiny little rhinestones on each side. "I apologize if that's how you construed it," she said. "It was never about reinvention. You're a very special person, Jessie Ivy. It would be a shame to reinvent yourself. It's about learning how to grow within yourself."

I felt my redheaded flush creeping up my cheeks when she called me *special*, but I still wasn't ready to give up. "So, doesn't that mean you want me to try new things?"

One corner of her mouth lifted, although I couldn't see what I'd said that was amusing. "In a way, you're right," she said. "But remember that it's not about what I want."

Yeah, yeah. We'd been over this before. "I know, it's about what I want," I said. That didn't seem totally true—there were a lot of people in my life who all had different ideas, from Mo, who wanted me to be an Elite gymnast, to Layla, who wanted me to do a double twist, to Mr. Freeman, who wanted me to be a student. So if the question was what *I* wanted, then the answer was simple. I wanted to make each of those people happy and proud of me.

At first, my birthday felt like any other day. I woke up with my muscles aching, my calves burning, as I pointed my toes underneath the bedspread. Then I smelled banana pancakes, a smell I would always associate with my birthday, since my mother always used to make them as a special birthday treat. Then, I'd been excited about the indulgence, but this morning my head felt woolly and I had a hard time mustering up any feelings stronger than irritation. I checked to see if I'd woken up on the wrong side of the bed, but I'd slept the way I generally did, spread almost diagonally, with my head closer to the wall and my feet hanging almost off the edge.

It was still dark outside, and usually my mother would have been sitting at the table, blearily sorting through the mail while she sipped her third cup of coffee. But today she was standing at the stove, humming to herself while she flipped pancakes. I climbed up onto one of the barstools at the granite counter and watched her cook.

"Are we going to have time?" I asked. We had to leave for the gym in twenty minutes, which didn't seem like enough time to eat breakfast. Usually, my mom gave me something to eat in the car on the way.

She turned around, sliding two pancakes onto a plate and passing it to me. "Happy birthday!" she said.

"Mom," I said. "I still have to get ready."

"You can take ten minutes to eat some pancakes," she said. "I put extra bananas in them, just like when you were little. Do you remember that?"

"Mom, I can't have pancakes before workout," I said. "They're nothing but empty carbs. I'll be starving by the time I get to school."

"I'll make you a hard-boiled egg," my mom said, crossing to the refrigerator. "Or would you like it scrambled?"

It was like she wasn't hearing me. "There's no *time*," I said again. "I'll just have an energy bar."

"Jessie," my mom said warningly, and I knew she was remembering a few months ago, when I'd started restricting what I ate to try to lose weight for gymnastics. I grabbed two energy bars, holding them up so she could see.

"I'll eat both of these in the car," I said. "You can watch me. But right now, I have to go get dressed."

"Okay," she said, spearing the two pancakes on my plate with a fork. She removed a plastic sandwich big from the drawer and slid the pancakes inside. "You can bring these, too; maybe you can have them for a snack later."

My mother had made me banana pancakes on every one of my birthdays for as long as I could remember, so I didn't know what was bothering me now. But for some reason, it grated on me that she was pushing this breakfast. I snatched the plastic bag from her hand, even though I had no intention of eating the pancakes now or later.

"I was thinking we could do something this weekend for your birthday," my mother said. "What about Sunday, when you have off from gym? You could invite your friends over, swim in the pool."

"Sure," I said, disappearing into my room to get dressed for gym. My mother followed me, talking through the door.

"Your dad wants to take you to dinner tonight," she said, "but I told him that was up to you. I could call in to work today, so I could drive you around and make you whatever you want for dinner. What about lemon pepper chicken? You love that."

I had thrown a pair of shorts over my leotard, and I had a bag packed with a change of clothes for school. I flung open the door to my room, and my mom stepped back.

Dr. Fisher had told me I needed to think about what I wanted, and so now I was ready to take a stand. "I'm having dinner with Dad tonight," I said. "You didn't tell him to cancel, did you?"

"No," she said, blinking at me. "Of course not."

"Good," I said, holding up my bag with my clothes and the little sandwich bag full of pancakes, so she wouldn't hassle me about them again. "Are we ready to go now?"

That night, I waited in the living room, where I could see out the front window to the driveway. My dad had said he would pick me up at seven, but it was seven thirty and he wasn't there yet. Deep down, I knew he probably wasn't coming, but I didn't want to get all worked up and mad, in case he did show up. It would be awful if I ruined the dinner by being upset.

My mom checked in on me periodically and said it wasn't too late for her to make the lemon pepper chicken. I felt bad about being so snippy with her earlier—she had only been trying to give me what she thought I would want. I couldn't fault her for that. At the same time, I didn't want to hear her say, *I told you so*, which was pretty much what she *was* saying every time she offered to turn on the oven and get the chicken roasting.

Then Rick came to tell me he'd heard them talking about Nadia Comaneci on SportsCenter. Usually, they only discussed baseball and football and basketball, so he knew I was always excited to hear about a gymnastics mention.

"What did they say?" I asked, although my heart wasn't in it.

He scratched his chin, looking up at the ceiling as though trying to remember. "Well, let's see," he said. "They were talking about a home-run hit by Evan Longoria, and they called it a perfect ten. That has to do with Nadia Comaneci, right? Didn't she get the first perfect ten?"

It was a stretch, but I gave him a little smile anyway. It was nice to know he listened to all the stuff I rambled on about at dinner sometimes.

Even Josh stopped on his way out the door to tell me happy birthday. "Maybe if I don't get home too late, we can play Super Mario on the Wii," he said. "How does that sound?"

I nodded, though I knew I'd probably be asleep by the time he got home, unless my dad showed up. At that point, if we went to dinner right away, it would have lasted past my usual bedtime. Not that I would have minded, of course.

"Do you want to open your birthday present?" Mom asked tentatively. "It might cheer you up."

Another way of saying, *I told you so*, but I decided to give her a break. "Sure," I said.

She left the room for a minute and returned with a small box, wrapped in bright pink paper and tied with a curling white ribbon. She handed it to me, taking a seat next to me on the couch.

I slid my finger under the seam in the paper, taking care to fold it back in a way that left the paper intact. I used to save all of my wrapping paper; I had red-and-white candy-cane stripes from Christmas, yellow with daisies from an Easter gift my grandmother had given me, and even some gymnastics-themed wrapping paper that my mom had specially ordered once online. I still remembered what had come in that package: my very own grips for the uneven bars, a sign that I was at a level high enough to need my own equipment—extra tools to help me swing higher and grip the bar better.

It was a jewelry box. I opened the velvet lid to reveal a pair of diamond earrings glittering up at me. And then suddenly, all I could see was a watercolor of that sparkle, prisms of yellow and pink and blue, and I realized I was crying.

"Do you like them?" my mom asked worriedly.

"They're beautiful," I said. I leaned my head against her chest until she brought her hand up to stroke my hair. It was like I was eight years old, but it felt good. I wanted to thank my mom, tell her that I loved the gift, apologize to her for the way I'd acted earlier that morning. But the lump in my throat was too huge, and so instead all I said was, "Lemon pepper chicken sounds nice. You know, if it's not too late to make it."

I felt my mother smiling into my hair. "It's not too late," she said.

Nine

My mom had said I could have a
pool party for my birthday, so I invited
Noelle, Christina, and Britt over to
my house on Sunday. But then I'd been at cheer
practice—my compromise with Mo was that I only
attended one cheer practice a week, instead of two,
so I didn't miss so many gymnastics sessions—and
somehow I'd found myself inviting Layla, Stephenie,
and Ashley, too. I was a little nervous about how
everyone would interact, given the age differences
and the fact that neither group really knew the other.

Christina and Noelle were the first to arrive,
and they started stripping down to their bathing

suits as soon as their feet hit the linoleum, with the ease of those who had been to my house many times before.

"Let's go swimming, already," Christina said. "She is driving me crazy."

"Who?" I glanced at Noelle, even though it seemed highly unlikely that it would be her. Noelle was like the patron saint of patience. Maybe it was from having to watch her little brothers or work at her parents' store all the time, but she always managed to keep her cool.

"My mother, of course," Christina said. "Who do you think?"

Christina constantly complained about her mother, even though Mrs. Flores seemed awesome to me. She was superdevoted to Christina's gymnastics and was willing to do anything or pay any expert it took to help Christina succeed. Not that my own family wasn't also supportive, but my mom had her job, and Rick mostly talked about gymnastics in baseball analogies, and Josh and Tiffany seemed mostly to think it was really weird that I spent so much time on this sport. Christina's mom not only accepted Christina's dream, she actively participated in it.

Still, I'd known Christina for a long time, and so I knew that she was prone to being dramatic. Sometimes it was best just to smile and nod rather than rile her up.

"Enough about my crazy family," Christina said. "Boring! Let's talk about Noelle's instead. How's your cute brother, Noelle? Still single?"

I didn't know if Christina actually thought Noelle's older brother, Mihai, was cute, or if she just said it to fluster Noelle. Either way, it was one thing guaranteed to challenge Noelle's patience.

"Gross!" Noelle said. "Seriously, quit it. Why don't you ever ask Jessie inappropriate questions about Josh?"

"Hey," I said, "don't drag me into this. I do not know anything about my stepbrother's love life, and I would like to keep it that way, thank you very much."

Christina flipped her long black hair over one shoulder. "Whatever," she said. "I'm ready to swim. First one in the pool gets to be Mihai's girlfriend!"

Christina was off, and Noelle's naturally competitive spirit made her start to race across the living room before Christina's words actually sank in. She slowed down before she got to the open doors leading to the pool. "Cut it out!" she called as Christina dove into the crystal-clear water.

Christina emerged a moment later, grinning, her hair splayed out like a mermaid's. "You know I'm just teasing. Come on, the water's great." She called to me, still standing by the front door. "What are you waiting for, birthday girl? It's not a party without you."

Just then, the doorbell rang; I thought I knew who it was. I glanced back and saw that Noelle was wading into the pool. I hoped that both she and Christina would stay occupied long enough for me to get Layla and her posse into the house without awkwardness.

"Hi, guys," I said, holding the door open for them to enter. "Welcome to my party."

I hoped that that didn't sound as dumb to them as it did to me. I didn't have little candy party favors or anything like that. Although maybe I should've gotten some of those. Everyone liked candy, after all.

I held my breath as Layla surveyed the house with that bored expression she seemed to wear half the time. "Swank digs," she said finally, and I exhaled.

"Thanks," I said. It wasn't a penthouse on Central Park, but I lived in a pretty nice gated community, and we had a maid come once a week to make sure the house stayed clean.

"The pool's this way," I said, gesturing toward the French doors leading out to the screened-in porch. "Can I get you anything to drink?"

Britt arrived while I was fetching their bottles of water, and I almost dropped them when she appeared at my elbow. I'd been holding one in each hand and had a third tucked under my arm, until Britt took one from me and eased the load.

"Tiffany let me in," she said. "Is she ever *not* on the phone?"

"I think she's seeing a doctor about having it surgically attached to her ear," I said. Britt grinned. I smiled back. Usually, Britt was the comedian, so it felt nice to be the one with the quip for once.

"I can hold my breath for almost two full minutes now," Britt was saying as we made our way to the porch. "I've been practicing in the bathtub. My grandmother says that if I need something to occupy me for two minutes, she can give me something, but I pointed out that this was going to make me an excellent scuba diver one day. Then she said that scuba divers have tanks, but—"

She stopped when she saw Layla, Stephenie, and Ashley on the lounge chairs by the pool. Christina and Noelle were awkwardly treading water in the deep end, looking everywhere but at us.

"Who are they?" Britt asked. I should've known she would cut right to the chase.

Britt didn't censor herself—she didn't know how to. Christina could be fairly blunt herself, but for some reason, even she was looking a little intimidated at the sight of the new girls. A small part of me took a weird satisfaction from that. Christina was so used to being the pretty one, the forceful one, that it was kind of gratifying to see that even she could be unsettled by these older girls.

"This is Layla," I said, gesturing toward her as she lazily rubbed sunscreen on her arms. She was barely covered by her small orange bikini, and I had to look away. She was like a girl in one of those lotion advertisements: smooth, perfect skin, and not a blemish in sight.

"And Stephenie and Ashley," I added. They gave halfhearted waves and returned to the magazines they must've brought with them, since we didn't usually keep any reading material out there.

"And these are my teammates at Texas Twisters, Christina and Noelle and Britt," I said, pointing to each of them in turn. Noelle said a small hello, but Christina's head disappeared under the water; when she came back up for air, she still wasn't looking at me.

"They're from cheerleading," I explained to Britt.

"I figured," she said. She set one of the bottles of water next to Layla, and I set the other two down on the table by Stephenie and Ashley. Britt gave me an unreadable look before shimmying out of her shorts to reveal her turquoise one-piece underneath. I was so used to seeing her with her hair up in a ponytail that seeing it down around her face was disconcerting because I couldn't see her expressive face to tell what she was thinking.

"My mom's making a parfait," I said, and could've slapped myself. It felt like everything I said sounded childish.

"A *what*?" Layla asked.

"Parfait," I repeated, a little more quietly. I didn't know if she was incredulous at the choice of dessert, or if she just really didn't know what it was. I assumed the former, since even McDonald's had parfaits now.

Britt, however, had no reservations about calling her out. "You layer fruit and yogurt," she said, in the same tone you might use to say, *A square has four sides, you idiot.*

Stephenie flipped her hair and leaned over to Ashley as if Britt hadn't spoken. "What kind of self-tanner do you use? It's not streaky at all."

Layla smiled, her white teeth gleaming in her tanned face, and jumped in to answer. "I used to use that brand with the dancing starfish in the commercial, but then I switched. . . ." And they were off, talking about boring stuff I didn't understand.

"So why are they here?" Britt asked me in that stage whisper of hers. I didn't say anything, but instead started to dip my toe in the shallow end of the pool, testing its temperature.

"You can sit over with us, Jessie," Layla said, indicating an empty chair. "There's a lot to talk about, with winter Sectionals coming up."

I hesitated. I didn't really want to leave my friends in the pool by themselves, but I liked the idea of putting off actually stripping down to my bathing suit. Even though I was in my leotard more hours of the day than not, I still felt vulnerable at the idea of standing there in front of Layla and the others wearing nothing but my yellow polka-dotted one-piece.

Britt stared at me. I bit my lip, and she turned her back on me. "Cannonball!" she shouted, running and doing a tucked front flip into the deep end of the pool.

I would just sit with Layla for a few minutes, I told myself—long enough to make her feel comfortable—and then I could join my teammates, who were splashing around in the pool. After all, Layla was my teammate now, too.

The week after my disastrous party—Layla, Stephenie, and Ashley had left before dessert, and it had been awkward after that with the others—Christina and Noelle left for the training camp. Because they'd both made the top ten, they were now invited to a special camp with National team coach Piserchia, who would select the six girls to compete at the USA vs. the World event.

In their absence, Britt and I mostly trained side by side in silence, which was weird, because Britt was *never* silent. If she wasn't whispering in my ear about how pointless a particular stretch was, she was cracking me up with a rant asking why they couldn't invent a leotard that didn't give you an instant wedgie. I'd apologized about the last-minute additions to the party, and Britt had shrugged and accepted it.

"They're your friends," she said. "You can invite who you want."

She said it matter-of-factly, as though she really didn't care, but she was also more distant with me now at the gym. So, when Layla called me up the next Sunday and asked if I wanted to go with her to the mall, I didn't hesitate. It wasn't like I had anyone else to hang out with. My stepsister acted like I was a germ on a kitchen sponge, Christina and Noelle were out of town, and I felt disconnected from Britt lately.

The mall was packed, so my mom dropped me off in front of the Food Court, where I was supposed to meet Layla. I half expected Stephenie and Ashley to be there, too, but when I walked through the glass doors I saw Layla standing alone, texting on her phone.

"I wanted to hang out with just you," she said when I asked about them. I was still glowing from that when she abruptly suggested that we get our picture taken.

I didn't have time to protest or ask any questions

as Layla pulled me by the arm behind the curtain of one of those freestanding photo booths. She swiped her credit card and tapped through the menu items with one blue-polished nail so quickly it was obvious she was an old pro.

"Smile," she commanded. I saw that she'd selected "Friends Forever," with a heart frame around our faces, so it wasn't hard for me to obey. Two seconds later, there was a clicking sound, and then a countdown began on the screen. "Now do something silly," she said.

When the pictures had printed out, she ripped one side off for me, accidentally tearing the bottom picture a little, and kept the untorn half for herself. I didn't have a purse or anything to put my strip of pictures in, but I didn't want them to get bent or messed up, so I just held them in my hand as we started walking through the mall. It felt like everything was happening very fast.

I wanted to ask Layla, *Why me?* She said she'd picked me for the cheerleading squad because of my tumbling skills, but I didn't get why she was so eager to be friends with me outside of that. She only took two friends a year to her dad's penthouse, after all, and she already had two perfect sidekicks in

Stephenie and Ashley. Only a few weeks ago, she'd been laughing at me in this very mall, and now she was linking her arm with mine as I stared down at the images of our two happy faces, pushed together in the confines of the photo booth.

"How often do you hang out with your gymnastics friends?" she asked.

"Well, we see each other practically every day in the gym," I said. "But that keeps us so busy we don't get together much outside of it." I thought about Britt's coming over during the first week of school, the way she'd stopped short of saying anything about my dad's birthday card, even though I knew she had an opinion.

"Hmm," Layla said, stopping in front of a store window. It was so sudden that I was yanked forward by her arm, still linked with mine, and would've tripped if I hadn't caught myself in time.

"That's what we *have* to be for Halloween," she said. I followed her gaze to see a short black dress, made of a shiny fabric underneath black lace.

"Um . . . what?" I asked. People going to a cocktail party? Goth celebrities? I didn't understand what the costume was.

But Layla was already pulling me into the store.

"Vampires," she said. "It's all the rage right now."

"That dress doesn't really look vampirey," I said.

"With fake fangs and the right makeup, it will," she said gleefully, making a beeline for the rack where the dress was hanging in all different sizes.

"You're a small?" she guessed, eyeing me. I thought about what my mom said, about always trying clothes on, but I was afraid to mention anything in case Layla remembered that mortifying incident with the bras. Though maybe she'd forgotten all about it.

"I guess," I said, and she yanked one off the rack for me.

Layla paid for three dresses for her and Stephenie and Ashley, leaving me to pay for mine. It was forty dollars, which was all the money my mother had given me to spend at the mall, but I didn't mind. It felt like I was buying a ticket to fun Halloween plans, which was worth every penny.

"Do you have any heels?" Layla asked. I started to say that I had a pair of platform sandals that I'd worn to the postparade reception just a little while ago, but she cut me off. "What am I thinking? Of course you don't. Let's go find you some."

"I have heels," I said quickly, thinking of the twenty-eight cents in my pocket.

"Oh, my God," Layla said, and this time I waited to see what she was exclaiming over. I'd already learned that she had a very short attention span, and that being with her was like being with a toddler all hopped up on sugar. I'd only been in the mall for half an hour, but I felt tired, like I'd been doing vault timers, sprinting down the runway and hitting the horse over and over.

"Is that *Norman,* from school?" she said, and I looked to where she was pointing.

I saw the carousel spinning in the center of the mall and heard kids screeching with glee as the horses rose up and down in time to the music. My eyes scanned the kiosks where they were selling personalized miniature license plates, butterfly wings, and wigs, but I didn't see Norman. "Where?"

"There," she said, pointing at the carousel. I squinted, and then I saw him, but only for an instant; he was on the back of a dark horse, one hand holding on to his glasses as he disappeared around the other side only to reappear again a few seconds later. He looked like he was having fun.

"I think so," I said.

"Are you guys friends?" Layla asked me. "I see you talking to him in homeroom sometimes."

Even though I mostly hung out with Layla, Ashley, and Stephenie in homeroom now, I still talked to Norman once in a while. He wasn't in any of my classes, probably because he was in the most advanced classes and I was mainly in regular ones.

"Not really," I said, but I wondered how he would answer the same question. Did he consider me a friend? I bet he would have said yes.

"He is so weird," Layla said. I squelched the disloyalty I felt as I agreed with her.

The carousel stopped, and there was a flood of children as they all joined their parents on the ground. Norman stuck out like a sore thumb, taller and gawkier than anyone else there.

Layla tugged on my shirtsleeve. "Come on," she said.

I didn't ask her where we were going, but I wasn't surprised when we intercepted Norman by the Whimsical Flights of Fancy kiosk.

"Hey, Abnorman," Layla said, bumping him with her shoulder. I was beginning to see that this was Layla's thing: she liked to accidentally-on-purpose knock into people. It made me rethink my original name for her, Watch-It Girl. She'd told *me* to watch it, but obviously she was the one who created all of these run-ins.

"Hi, Layla," Norman said, ignoring the nickname. His eyes lit up when he saw me. "Hey, Jessie."

"Hi," I said.

"Shopping for your Halloween costume?" Layla asked, smirking meaningfully in the direction of the wispy dress-up butterfly wings at the kiosk, which were colored bright pink and purple.

"No," he said. "I don't really think that children younger than one year or older than twelve years should trick-or-treat. Although I did once have an old man dressed as Mr. Burns from *The Simpsons* come to my house and ask for candy. True story. I think the liver spots were real."

Layla curled her lip. "I just figured, since you love rides meant for three-year-olds, that you'd want to dress like one, too."

"Carousels transcend age," Norman said grandly. "Did you guys get your picture taken?"

He was looking at the photo strip I still held. I quickly dropped my hand. For some reason, I didn't want him to see the pictures of Layla and me acting silly together, our faces framed by big red hearts.

Norman smiled politely at me, and Layla, watching the exchange, laughed. "You're right," she said to me. "He *is* weird."

My gaze flew to Norman, hoping he didn't think I had really said that. I mean, I *had* said it, but it wasn't like I'd said it first. I was just agreeing with Layla. I'd told myself that Norman would probably have acknowledged that fact about himself. He seemed like the type of person who would own his weirdness—who would prefer being different over being another clone.

But Norman had taken his glasses off and was cleaning the lenses with the bottom of his T-shirt, so all I could see was the top of his head. He had a little bit of dandruff in his hair, I saw, and for one instant he glanced up without his glasses, and it was as though his face was oddly naked. But then he put his glasses back on, and he was just Norman.

"Well," he said, not meeting my gaze, "I have to go. Have fun shopping."

And then he disappeared among the throng of people walking through the mall. I thought of Layla's earlier question: I'd been sure that Norman would have said I was a friend. Now I wasn't so sure. Even though I'd said before that I didn't consider him a friend, I couldn't think of any other way to explain the sudden hole that I felt open up inside me, as though I'd lost something before I'd had the chance to appreciate it.

Ten

Because I'd spent most of my only day off at the mall and then hanging out with Layla at her gigantic house, I hadn't finished my American Government homework. So I was busily copying questions from the book when Norman walked into homeroom, sliding his rolling backpack up to his desk.

"What are you doing?" he asked.

It was pretty obvious, but I still felt bad about what had happened at the mall, and I didn't need another person mad at me. I tucked my hair behind my ear and tried to hold on in my mind to the sentence I had been about to write as I answered him.

"Mr. Freeman's homework," I said.

"Ah," he said. "Checks and balances. The legislative, executive, and judicial branches. The foundation of democracy."

"What?" I said. I was watching the door, trying to see if Layla and her posse had walked in yet.

"So, you haven't gotten that far," Norman said. "Well, don't worry about it. There's a sub today."

I dropped my pencil in relief. "Thank God."

He eyed my paper, with its barely legible handwriting. Mr. Freeman required us to copy down all of the questions and then respond in complete sentences, so I'd been scribbling my fastest, trying to complete everything in time. I was sure that Norman could tell just by looking at it that I hadn't done a very good job. Each of his answers was probably a paragraph long, whereas mine only took up a couple of lines.

"Busy weekend?" he asked. I couldn't tell if he was sarcastically referring to my trip to the mall, or if he was genuinely curious.

"Yeah," I said. "I have this Elite qualifier coming up soon, so I'm training pretty hard for it. I spent most of Saturday in the gym."

"You have to be Elite to go to the Olympics,

right?" he said. "So would that make you a Level Ten now, technically?"

I gave him a surprised smile. "I didn't know you were a gymnastics fan," I said.

His prominent Adam's apple bobbed in his throat as he swallowed. "Wikipedia," he said. "I did some research."

"Not bad," I said. "Yeah, I have to make the Elite team if I even want a chance at competing at the next Olympics. Not that I think I have a shot."

Layla entered the room in a flurry of chatting and giggling with Stephenie and Ashley, but I didn't feel like ending my conversation with Norman, so I avoided their gaze. "Two of my teammates are competing in this international competition next week," I said. "They're in the top ten gymnasts in the country, and I found out this morning that they impressed the National team coach enough to go to San Jose. Now, *that's* cool."

"You'll make it there someday," Norman said, and even though he had never seen me compete and knew nothing about my scores or my skills, I appreciated his having confidence in me.

I was excited for Christina and Noelle, who were flying directly from the National team camp in Houston to San Jose. I didn't even think I was jealous anymore. After all, I had a whole other life now outside of gymnastics. I still loved the sport— I always would. But I felt like I was growing apart from it, little by little, as though I was carving out something else with Layla and the cheerleading squad.

I finally glanced over at Layla, who raised her eyebrows with a meaningful look at Norman. I picked up my pencil and focused on the paper in front of me, as though I'd been doing homework all along.

I felt Norman's gaze on me. "Checks and balances," he said. "You'll get to it. It's where one branch has to limit the other, so that power doesn't get corrupted. It's actually quite pertinent to high school."

Mr. Freeman returned the next day, and when I handed in my homework, he passed back the previous assignment. A big red number sixty-seven was at the top of the page. *See me*, a note said.

I waited until the other students were filing out of the classroom, and then I approached his desk. I hoped that maybe it had all been a mistake—that maybe he had switched my grade with someone else's in the class—but as soon as he looked up at me, I knew that that wasn't the case.

"Miss Ivy," he said. "Thank you for seeing me."

You told me to, I thought, but I didn't say anything.

"Do you know why you got such a low grade?" Mr. Freeman asked. When I just stared back at him, he answered his own question. "You parroted back the information from the chapter, but you didn't add any of your own voice."

He took the paper from my limp fingers, pointing to one of the questions. "Here, for example," he said. "You cite the court case that upheld Congress's implied powers. That's good, but it can be easily looked up in the book. It's even bolded, to make it easier to find. The question asks you to give an example of an implied power, and assess *why* Congress should have such power."

I'd done that assignment late one night, after a long day of gymnastics, school, then back to gymnastics, before heading out to cheerleading practice and coming home just in time to eat a leftover Caesar salad from the fridge and go to bed. There was even a spot on the edge of the paper that

I knew was Caesar dressing. I'd tried unsuccessfully to wipe it off before I turned it in.

"Sorry," I mumbled. "There's this Elite qualifier coming up—"

But Mr. Freeman held up his hand. "Believe me, Jessie, I get it," he said. "I played college football for the University of Texas, where we had to keep our grades up if we wanted to stay on the team."

I hadn't known that. It made sense, though, since he was so tall.

"Now, I know your gymnastics isn't directly tied to the school," he said. "But just as your coach holds you to a high standard in the gym, I hold you to a high standard in here. Understand?"

I nodded, trying to blink away the tears that were stinging my eyes. After weeks in the gym, I still wasn't doing any better with skills like my double tuck front on floor. I hated the thought that I was messing up in school, too.

"You've joined the cheerleading team, too, is that right?" Mr. Freeman asked.

I nodded again, and this time a single tear slipped down my cheek. I didn't wipe it away, hoping that Mr. Freeman wouldn't notice.

He hesitated. "You might be spreading yourself

a little thin," he said. "Perhaps you need to think about your priorities."

It wasn't the first time I'd heard that, but I still didn't appreciate everyone telling me how to live my life. "Are we done?" I asked stiffly.

He sighed, handing my paper back to me. "Do you know Norman Coswell? He and a few other students are organizing a study session this Saturday for the midterm. If you're able to attend, it might help you to prepare."

"Okay," I said, although I had no intention of asking Norman about it. Saturday was the USA vs. the World event, and there was a gathering at the gym for everyone to watch Christina and Noelle compete. I had to be there.

But I knew better than to bring that up to Mr. Freeman, who already questioned my priorities. I left the classroom just as other students were coming in for the next period, and I crumpled the paper in my hand, throwing it in the trash can.

Eleven

Mo had gotten flags representing all of the countries competing in the USA vs. the World event and hung them around the gym. She'd also rented a projector, and so the entire competition would be shown on one of the white concrete-brick walls of the gym, almost like in a movie theater.

Britt and I hadn't been on great terms since my birthday party, but at least we could connect over how cool it was to get a break from training to watch the competition on TV. It felt weird to be sitting on one of the benches usually reserved for parents watching their kids practice as we ate air-popped popcorn and apple slices while they showed the usual fluff about each of the athletes.

The announcers barely even mentioned Noelle and Christina, but then, that wasn't surprising. Mostly, people were interested in the Senior girls who were competing, since they were at the Olympic level and they were the big names. I'd even heard a rumor that one of the girls was going to appear on *Dancing with the Stars*.

"Do you know what the implied powers of Congress are?" I asked Britt during the first commercial break. I didn't really care; I just wanted to break the ice, and it was the first thing I thought of.

She considered the question. "It's something about being necessary and proper," she said. "I remember my grandmother talking about it when we went to D.C. one summer. It's kind of like this catchall clause that means they can do whatever they want."

"Well, then, how does that figure into checks and balances?" I asked.

Britt shrugged. The commercial break ended, and we watched one of the Senior Chinese girls mount the balance beam. She pushed herself up into a one-armed handstand, holding that position for a ridiculously long time before lowering herself to the beam and continuing her routine.

"Wow," I said. I had forgotten that it was stuff like that that had made me fall in love with gymnastics in the first place—a move that seemed impossible, until someone found a way to do it, and then someone else found a way to make it even harder and more impressive a few years later. I thought of the full-twisting basket toss that Layla and the girls were trying to get and wondered if they felt the same way about cheerleading. So far, I hadn't gotten to try anything except tumbling back and forth and learning a couple of their basic chants.

"I should've told you that I was inviting those girls to my party," I blurted out.

"Why *did* you invite them?" Britt asked. "They were kind of snotty."

I could see how they could seem that way if you didn't know them. I still didn't feel totally comfortable around Stephenie and Ashley, who mostly ignored me. But now that I'd spent some time with her, I could see that Layla could be really nice. She'd bought me a lip gloss at the mall, because, she'd said, it was a crime for lips to be as dry as mine were, and she was always including me in her plans now, like when she thought up those Halloween costumes. It felt nice to be included.

"Cheerleading is really fun," I said, instead of addressing Britt's question directly. "I think you'd like it."

A group of Level Seven girls needed to pass by to find seats, so Britt and I stood up, leaning as far back as we could to make space. After we'd sat back down, it was a few minutes before Britt picked up the conversation again.

"I don't know," she said. "I don't really see the point. Don't get me wrong, I've seen all the Bring It On movies, and they're pretty cool. But it seems to me like we already get to do the best parts of cheerleading every day: the tricks and jumps and flips. So why would I want to bother with yelling at some football player to go for the goal? I don't care about that."

"There's more to it than that," I protested. If Britt had decided to try something new, I would've been nothing but supportive about it. So I didn't see why I was getting so much flak from everyone—Britt, Mo, Mr. Freeman.

Britt looked like she was about to say something else when I saw Noelle's image projected on the wall, and we all cheered. She looked different somehow blown up like that, but at the same time, like the quiet, serious Noelle I'd known for years. I realized that I did miss her and Christina; ever since I started high school, I'd felt like I hadn't seen as much of my old teammates as I used to, or at least that our friendships had been somehow altered.

Mo gestured for everyone to hush so that we could hear the audio.

"Noelle Onesti, from Austin, Texas, is the current Junior National Champion on the balance beam," one announcer said, and then the other, a woman who was an ex-gymnast herself, added, "You're going to see a lot of exciting gymnastics from this young dynamo."

"Dynamo?" Britt repeated. "Noelle's awesome, don't get me wrong, but *dynamo*? I don't know if that's how I'd describe her style of gymnastics. Dynamite's like an explosion—*bam!*—and she's more precise than that. She thinks about every tiny detail."

I shot Britt a sidelong look. "Let me guess," I said. "You think *you're* more the dynamo type."

She tossed her white-blond head. "*I* wouldn't necessarily say that," she said. "But since *you* did, then sure. I think that's a fair assessment."

Britt grinned at me. It felt good to have my friend back. But it also got me thinking about how I'd be described, if I were ever actually to be featured on TV. My gymnastics wasn't as breath taking as Britt's; she was so tiny that she could really fly. And I definitely wasn't as graceful as Christina, who actually spent her Sundays off working out at a ballet studio and had the most perfect toe point I'd ever seen. Then there was Noelle, who Britt was totally right about. Noelle considered all the little details. Even now, as I watched her dance across the length of the balance beam, I could close my eyes and picture every single move in her routine, because she had done it so consistently again and again.

"How would you describe me?" I asked Britt.

"Uh, red hair," Britt said. "Obviously. Freckles, although I know you hate them. Really pretty green eyes . . ."

"Thanks," I said, blushing at the compliment. "But my gymnastics, I mean. How would you describe my gymnastics?"

"You're powerful," she said. It was true that vault was usually my best event, and I'd gotten the speed and height to do a Yurchenko faster than either Noelle or Christina, but that word still felt to me like a euphemism for *stocky*. Because I had an athletic body type, everyone assumed I was powerful.

"Then how come I can't seem to get my double front?" I asked. "A 'powerful' gymnast should be able to land that, no problem, but I always come up short."

"You'll get it," she said. But as we both turned back to watch Noelle execute a flawless dismount, it occurred to me that Britt hadn't really answered my question.

Over the next couple of weeks, Mr. Freeman reviewed material for the midterm we had coming up. I tried to pay attention, because I knew I would need the information, but it was hard to focus on concepts that didn't even affect me, when there was so much other stuff going on in my life. Sometimes I thought I was listening and then found myself staring out the window twenty minutes later, when class was dismissed, and I couldn't remember how I'd gotten that way.

"Jessie?" Mr. Freeman said. I realized he'd called my name a couple of times. Everyone in class was staring at me. I brought my hand down from my chin so fast that it slammed against the desk.

It was hard to read Mr. Freeman's gaze, but I imagined I could see that big red sixty-seven reflected in his eyes. "I asked you to define the implied powers of Congress," he said.

I knew we'd been over this a million times, and I was pretty sure I knew what the implied powers were. But I couldn't put my finger on it just then, with everyone looking at me—with *him* looking at me. "Um . . . they're, like, extra powers. Congress has certain powers, and then they have these extra ones."

That must've been close enough, because he nodded slightly. But before I could relax, he asked, "And what is one example of an implied power?"

I knew we had gone over this, too, and could even remember Mr. Freeman's drawing something on the board. But I couldn't remember what that something was, which was the really important part. "I don't know," I said finally, figuring it was better to admit it than to make a far-off guess that would only embarrass me.

His gaze was level with mine for a moment, and then he went to the whiteboard, drawing a big rectangle with a dollar sign in each corner and a squiggly George Washington head in the middle. Now I remembered his drawing that. He liked to scribble little doodles on the board to help us to learn certain terms or examples. George Washington's profile had looked just as deflated the first time as it did now.

"Money," he said, addressing the entire class. "Banks. Congress has the expressed power—that means it's in the Constitution—to print currency, which means that it's *implied* that they have the power to form a national bank to store that currency. That's only one example, but you might want to keep it in mind, as you never know if it'll show up on the test or not."

He winked, and several people snickered. I slouched down in my seat, anxious for the class to end.

When the bell finally rang, I hurried to scoop up my books, in a rush to get out of there before Mr. Freeman could pull me aside. Unfortunately, I wasn't fast enough. I felt my ears burn as he walked up and leaned over my desk to ask if we could have a little chat.

I didn't know why he was bothering to ask, since I couldn't really say no. "Okay," I said.

"I'm just worried about your grade," he said. "I know you're usually a good student, but this midterm is not going to be easy. And if you fail it, it'll be hard for you to recover before report-card time."

"I'll know all of these definitions by then," I said. "I promise."

He leaned against one of the desks, placing his hand on the wooden surface, which was covered with scratched-in initials. "That's what I'm telling you. It's not going to be enough to memorize. You're going to have to be able to tell me things like *why* these implied powers are important. Do you know the answer to that?"

I really wanted to turn around and run, especially because I knew that the students from the next class would be showing up soon. But I was also determined to get this question right, to prove to Mr. Freeman that I wasn't some jock who didn't have a brain. So I paused, giving it some thought before answering him.

"Well, the Constitution can't cover everything, so the implied powers exist to fill in the blanks. Otherwise, our country would be stuck, unable to proceed with anything. Like that example about the banks."

Mr. Freeman drummed with his fingers on the desk. "Exactly," he said. "But they're dangerous, too. Sometimes it's easy to say that the end always justifies the means, but that kind of free rein can be a slippery slope. We might say that the government's ability to regulate banks is a good thing, but where do we draw the line at what the government can do with our money? Or with anything else? Do you believe the end always justifies the means?"

I didn't know how he wanted me to answer that one, so I just blurted out, "Yes."

For a moment, he looked truly disappointed. Defeated, even. But then the door burst open, a crush of chattering students poured into the classroom, and he stood up. "I know you've been working toward one goal your whole life," he said. "Just keep in mind that there are many ways to get there, okay? Some better than others. And try to pay more attention in class."

I promised, but I would've said anything to get out of there. I had too many other things to worry about without Mr. Freeman's cryptic little statements bouncing around in my head.

Twelve

When Britt called on Halloween night, I was standing in front of the mirror in my room, slicking lip gloss on with my finger. I'd tried to apply it directly from the stick but kept smearing it on my teeth or in the corner of my mouth. I thought about asking Tiffany to help me, but didn't want to risk her laughing at me when she saw me in my tight black dress.

I didn't even check the screen before answering my cell phone, and was surprised to hear Britt's voice.

"What's up?" she said.

"Oh, um . . ." I tried to think of something to

say. Even though Britt and I were doing a lot better after the USA vs. the World event, it was still awkward to talk about the cheerleading squad with her.

"Christina and Noelle just got back," Britt said. "And we were thinking about all hanging out for Halloween at Christina's house. We don't need to trick-or-treat or anything like that, since we can't eat any of the stuff anyway. But we'll still dress up; watch a movie or something."

"I don't have a costume," I said, cringing at my reflection. Layla was going to do the vampire makeup at her house, so right now I looked like I was going to a club instead of out for Halloween. I'd have to wrap myself in a coat before I stepped out of my house, or else my mom would never let me leave.

"That's okay," Britt said. "We don't really, either. Christina is wearing a flapper dress from last year, and Noelle has a traditional Romanian skirt that her aunt sent her. It's pretty warm out tonight, so I may just go as a gymnast, with one of my leotards and a pair of workout shorts."

"I don't know," I began, but Britt was still talking.

"—Back home, I always went as a gymnast," she

continued, "because then, if they asked me to do a trick, I could do a standing back tuck, which was good for another candy bar, easy. Of course, that was back when I used to be able to *eat* candy."

"I think I may stay here," I said, "I'm not feeling that well."

There was a pause on the other end of the line. "Okay," Britt said. "Well, if you change your mind . . . call Christina."

"I will," I promised. I snapped my cell phone shut, staring back at the strange girl in the mirror with her straightened red hair and shiny pink lips. Even without the fangs, I already felt like I was in costume.

"Your hair is awesome," Layla gushed when she showed up at my door. Her older sister was waiting impatiently at the curb, her car idling.

"Thanks," I said. I did think I looked fairly good, for once. The hair made me seem older, less like Little Orphan Annie and more like a grown-up. "I borrowed my stepsister's hair straightener."

I didn't know if *borrowed* was the right term. I had given it back, but then again, she didn't know I had taken it in the first place, and she'd have been livid if she'd found out I had invaded her space. I'd been worried I would fry a strip of my hair off, but in the end it wasn't that hard to figure out: I just dragged the straightener through my hair until the strands lay flat.

I called out a quick good-bye to my mother over my shoulder, and then I was climbing into Layla's sister's car, wedging myself into the backseat between Stephenie and Ashley.

"We were talking about hitting up Spanish Trace," Layla said, naming the swanky subdivision where Christina lived.

I paused in the act of buckling my seat belt. "Why would we go there?" I asked, my voice squeaking a little. "I mean, your neighborhood is really nice. Or we could even trick-or-treat around here."

"No offense, but this neighborhood is mostly old people," Layla said, turning in her seat and catching Stephenie's gaze; Stephenie laughed. "And I live on like, three acres. It's too spread out. Spanish Trace has the best candy; I heard they give away whole Three Musketeers bars."

"*Not* that you can afford to eat many of those if you want to do your basket toss," Ashley pointed out. Layla shot her a nasty glare.

"I'm not going to stuff myself the way you do," Layla said. "Although you have ways of taking care of that, don't you?"

Ashley just narrowed her eyes and stared out the window, ignoring Layla. I glanced between the two of them, wondering what the history was there. Was it possible that Ashley had struggled with her own eating problems, the way I had? Maybe that was something we could connect over and talk about. It'd be nice to feel like I wasn't alone.

I asked Layla when she was going to do my vampire makeup, and she tossed back an opened package of face paints. "Just put the white all over your face, and use the red to make blood," she said. "Steph, let Jessie use your compact."

The passing cars' headlights revealed that Stephenie's and Ashley's makeup looked perfect—their faces were ghostly white, with thin drips of blood coming from their red lips. It occurred to me that I should've used a red lipstick instead of the pink lip gloss that Layla had given me. I'd been looking forward to Layla's doing my makeup for me, because I'd had so little experience with it myself, except for the small amount my mom put on me for competitions.

I thought suddenly of Britt and Noelle and Christina, who were probably getting ready right now. Britt would have done something crazy with her hair, like using temporary dye to put a blue streak in it, or putting it in a ponytail at the very top of her head. Christina would be pushing some mushy romantic movie, Britt would be fighting for horror, and Noelle would be trying to mediate the whole thing. It would be way more fun than what I was doing right now.

I felt disloyal again. After all, Layla hadn't *had* to invite me out tonight. She'd suggested that I wear this really pretty dress and included me in her group with its themed costumes. I couldn't complain about that. She considered *me* a friend—a friend forever, if the photo-booth pictures were to be believed.

So, when Layla's sister dropped us off at the gate leading to Christina's neighborhood, I vowed to be fun and interesting and to have a great time. And for the first twenty minutes, I did. We perfected our group pose for when people opened their doors, accepted our huge candy bars with smiles, and then giggled once they shut their doors, before moving on to the next house.

"These are going to help me with my PMS for the next year," Stephenie said, surveying her bag of chocolate.

"I don't know," Ashley said with a sly grin. "Aren't you PMS-ing like, twenty-four seven?"

Stephenie swung her bag at Ashley, who spun out of the way. "Shut up. If I'm in a bad mood when I'm around you, did you ever stop to think that maybe it's because I'm around you?"

"You guys already have your periods?" I asked. I couldn't believe that they were talking about PMS so casually, like it was just another part of life.

Layla stopped in the middle of the sidewalk, her black-rimmed eyes wide and incredulous. "You don't?"

I guess I should've expected that question. "I'm an athlete," I said awkwardly. "I train too hard for my body to get it, I think."

As soon as the words were out, I regretted them. I hadn't meant to imply that Layla was *less* of an athlete, just that when you trained like it was a full-time job, certain things were different. I knew that Tiffany got her period, because she would be all shifty-eyed when she had to throw a box of tampons in the shopping cart, especially when Rick was pushing it. But I'd never experienced even the slightest bit of spotting.

Then there was also the possibility that they would think I was a little kid, which was apparent when Ashley snickered. "Maybe Jessie's in the wrong costume," she said. "She should be wearing a bright orange pumpkin with felt leaves on it, like I did when I was seven."

Layla laughed, but oddly, it was Stephenie who stuck up for me. "Whatever," she said. "I would trade all of my *Twilight* stuff if it meant I didn't have to deal with that anymore. Seriously."

I hadn't expected Stephenie to come to my rescue, but I was glad she did, because it immediately defused some of the tension.

"She has a point," Layla agreed. "Periods can be such a pain."

Ashley motioned as if she were placing an invisible crown on her head. "Then crown me Queen Pain!" she said, and even I had to join in the laughter at that one. The rest of the time we spent trick-or-treating, I didn't even need to pretend to have fun. When Layla, Ashley, Stephenie, and I skipped down the sidewalk arm in arm, I wasn't pretending. I felt like I got what Dr. Fisher had been talking about. It *was* nice to have a different group of friends, friends I could relate to in a way that didn't always include gymnastics, and who could show me more about being a regular teenage girl.

Then came the moment I was dreading, when we approached Christina's house.

"Let's not go there," I said.

"Why not?" Layla asked. "This house is gigantic."

"It looks . . . haunted," I said, seizing on the only excuse I could think of. I could've kicked myself. I wasn't in an episode of *Scooby-Doo*.

Layla snickered. "Should I have gotten you cat ears instead of fangs?" she asked.

"Scaredy-cat," Stephenie said, as though I hadn't gotten the joke.

"Whatever," I said. "I have to make a quick phone call. My mom wanted me to check in."

Just shut up, Jessie. Everything I said made the situation worse. Now they were going to think I was a scaredy-cat who went crying to Mommy.

Layla glanced at Stephenie and Ashley and shrugged, and they started to walk away. I turned my back to them, making a show of digging through my little purse for my phone, even though I had no intention of calling her.

But then I heard Britt's voice, and my heart sank.

"Jessie?" She bounded down the front steps of the house but stopped at the bottom, before she reached me. I saw that her hair was crimped so that it stood around her head like a bunch of crinkly fries.

"I thought so," she said quietly. "I saw those girls at the door, and I had this sneaking suspicion that I'd find you out here. You're not here to hang out with us, are you?"

"I—"

"What are you wearing?" Britt asked, and the look she gave me made me feel as if I was wearing a giant sandwich board that said *Gymnastics Is for Losers* on it.

"You were the one who said we should reinvent ourselves, remember?" I blurted out. "You said it's a new school and a new year, and this is our chance to do something different."

"I meant, like, talk in an English accent for a day, because it'd be funny," Britt said. I couldn't remember ever seeing Britt angry; mostly, she treated everything like it was a big joke. But now, she was definitely mad. "I didn't mean *this*."

"That's easy for you to say," I said, getting irate

myself. "You know exactly who you are. You're the second-best gymnast in the country on vault. Who am I?"

"You're better than me on vault," Britt said, "and you know it. So don't make this about gymnastics when it's not."

"What does it matter?" I said. I wanted to yell, but I was keeping my voice no higher than a harsh whisper, so that Layla and the other girls didn't catch any of our argument. Stephenie and Layla were huddled around Ashley on the sidewalk inspecting a huge hole in Ashley's tights. I just hoped that that would occupy them long enough for me to handle this situation. "I'm not even an Elite yet, so no one knows whether I'm the best on vault or not. I might as well be nobody."

"If you really believe that," Britt said, "then I feel sorry for you."

She turned and stomped back up the steps to rejoin Christina and Jessie, who had just come out of the house and were staring at me. She glared at Layla as they passed each other. Layla glared back, before confronting me on the sidewalk.

"What is that girl's *problem*?" she said.

Me, I wanted to say. *That girl's problem is me.*

Thirteen

In homeroom on Monday morning, I was racing once again to finish my homework in time for Mr. Freeman's class. My mom had driven me from gym to school again, and since I'd told her I was finished with my homework, I couldn't very well do it in front of her. So now, I had twenty minutes to try to complete the whole assignment.

"Did you enjoy your All Hallows' Eve?" Norman asked as he fell into the seat in front of me. It seemed like Norman always made an entrance, like he couldn't stop himself from crash-landing into a scene.

"Yeah," I said, without looking up. In truth, it had been a crappy night. We'd trick-or-treated for another fifteen minutes after my confrontation with Britt, and then Layla had wanted us all to go somewhere else, but I'd begged off, citing early gym practice as a reason. So I had my mom pick me up, and I dodged her questions about why I was in Christina's neighborhood, and did I just want to spend the night and ride to gym with Christina in the morning? Finally, I gave my mom a Three Musketeers bar to silence her, and when I got home, I threw the rest of the candy in the pantry, where I knew Rick or Josh would find them.

During Saturday's practice, I tried to focus only on my gymnastics, since none of the other girls were going out of their way to talk to me. That was the funny thing about workouts: it could be easy to gloss over a falling-out. When we were all getting along, which was most of the time, we joked around a little and whispered to each other if Mo turned her back for a minute, but we still had to put most of our concentration into our reps. But if one of us was mad, it wasn't hard just to put your head down and pretend you were really, really working on improving your routines.

Not that mine was improving. I could land the double front okay on a softer mat, but ended up on my butt one out of every five times I attempted the pass, and the other four passes weren't exactly pretty. I felt Mo's gaze on me whenever I took my place in line to try again, but when I landed the pass—or especially when I didn't—I'd look up to find her paying attention to the Level Ten girls over on the balance beam, or strolling over to the front desk to talk to a parent.

I felt Norman's gaze on me now, and so I finally glanced up. "What?" I asked impatiently. In five minutes, we were all going to have to stand for the Pledge of Allegiance, which would cut into my homework time.

"I figured you would elaborate," he said, "but you didn't."

"You knew I was going out with Layla," I said. Layla, Stephenie, and Ashley were over in the corner, poring over some note Ashley had received from a boy. A part of me was happy to be left alone to work on my assignment and relieved that Layla didn't harass me about being friends with Norman anymore. But another part of me wondered if I was so unimportant, that Layla could act like we were best friends at cheerleading practice and then completely ignore me in homeroom.

"So, how was that?"

I felt like Norman knew somehow that the night hadn't exactly gone as planned, and his coyness irritated me. "It was fine," I snapped. "Listen, I really have to get back to this homework, okay? Mr. Freeman will jump down my throat if I get another bad grade."

"Ah," he said. "Jessie Ivy versus Mr. Freeman continues."

"Yeah," I said, "and I'm losing." And then I had an idea, one that normally would've never occurred to me, except that I was desperate. "Hey, maybe you could help me with this homework," I said. "You just came from this class."

"I hardly think there's enough time for a tutoring session," Norman said, pushing his glasses up the bridge of his nose with one finger.

"Well, not a tutoring session, exactly," I said.

"I'm not going to give you the answers," he said. "That's cheating. It's against the honor code. You can fail an assignment or even a class for that. True story."

"I didn't say to give me the answers," I said. I was conscious of the minutes ticking away. "But you could tell me where to find them in the book, maybe. It would help me get this done in time."

He looked at me for ten seconds. I knew precisely how long it was, because I was counting Mississippis in my head, wondering how many lines I could've written out by then.

"I can't do that," he said.

"Whatever," I said, returning pencil to paper. I knew I couldn't finish the whole thing in time by myself, but I wasn't going to force Norman to help me.

"You know," he said, "I thought you were different."

I didn't want to bite, but I couldn't let that comment go. "What does that mean?" I demanded.

"On the first day," he said, "I figured, here's someone who knows what it's like to be a little weird. You've been competing in gymnastics meets since you were seven—I know; I looked it up online."

I blinked at that. I couldn't believe he'd researched me.

"I memorized the periodic table when I was in fourth grade," Norman continued. "And I get it, no one wants to be friends with the guy who can recite every element and its atomic weight, but those same people don't seem to have a problem with using me to do their homework."

"I wasn't—" I began, but Norman shook his head.

"You *were*," he said. "And I thought you were better than that."

The morning announcements started, and Norman turned around to face the front. And even though I had a few more precious minutes while the anchors droned on about the lunch specials for the day, I couldn't concentrate on anything in my textbook. I stared at the bits of dandruff in Norman's hair and wondered if he knew that he had dandruff. Something told me that, even if he did, he wouldn't care what people thought of him for it. And then, for some reason, that reminded me of Britt's crazy, crimped hair on Halloween night, and it occurred to me that *she* hadn't cared if she looked ridiculous or not, either. I was the only one, with my hair that had taken an hour of straightening to tame, who had minded how people saw me.

The announcers on the morning show called for the Pledge of Allegiance, and so I forced all of those thoughts out of my head as I stood, putting my hand over my heart.

* * *

That Friday, I had to miss some gymnastics practice for a pep rally after school. It was my first time actually cheering with the team, and I was nervous.

I saw Norman in the bleachers as I marched out onto the basketball court with the rest of the squad, and I almost waved, before I remembered that he was mad at me. I don't know how I could've forgotten. It seemed like everyone was mad at me these days, except for Layla and the rest of the cheerleading team. Britt was still avoiding me, since Halloween; Mr. Freeman had handed back another paper with a big red F on it; and I knew Mo would be disapproving of the missed practice hours, given that the Elite qualifier was only two weeks away.

I took my place off to one side and crouched down until the tip of my ponytail brushed the floor. The song started—a grinding techno beat that I was already totally sick of—and I waited for my cue. But it was actually hard to make out the music, what with the crowd and the bad stereo system, and behind me, the routine sounded different from the way it did in practice. Everyone's tennis shoes squeaked on the polished wood, and the coach wasn't yelling out directions as she normally did. But then there was a cheer from the crowd, which told me that the three flyers had probably just been lifted for their first toss, and so I jumped up from my position and bounded into my tumbling.

I felt like clothes in a dryer, going end over end over end, one back handspring leading into another. I ended with the full twist and then launched into the same tumbling pass going back the other way. Once I'd reached the other side, the song was winding down, and I leapt up into a straddle jump. In cheerleading, they called it a toe-touch, but I was having a hard time with both the name and living up to the name. In gymnastics, you're not supposed to touch your toes when you jump up like that, and it was a difficult habit to break. Still, I knew that my straddle was the highest and my legs the straightest of anybody's, thanks to those ankle weights that Mo made us wear all the time.

We ended with a final pose, one hand on the hip and the other thrust into the air, holding up one finger. It was supposed to declare that our team was number one, but I thought it looked like we were trying to point out something on the ceiling, personally.

It only hit me as we were running off the court

that I'd just performed in front of the whole school. I'd competed in front of larger crowds than that before, like at the Texas State Championships the previous year, but it was different when it was all people your own age, whom you would potentially see again, rather than a bunch of parents of gymnasts from all over the state, who really didn't care what you were doing, as long as their daughter won a medal. Now, I couldn't remember if people had even clapped after our cheer. It felt as if I was just coming out of a vacuum of time and sound, and now I was trying to go back and figure out what had happened.

"Did people like it?" I asked Layla worriedly. "I heard them cheer once, but it all happened so fast. I've never . . ."

I almost said, *I've never felt so disconnected before*. And I realized it was true. When I competed in gymnastics, sometimes it felt a little surreal, just like it had out there today. But each move I did, down to even the minuscule dance moves I did to get from one end of the beam to the other, felt like *mine*. I felt aware of my body, of the experience of being out there on the floor or racing down the vault runway or letting go of the bar, spinning in the air, and catching it again. Today, I'd been more aware of how sweaty my armpits felt in the itchy long-sleeved shirt that was part of the cheer uniform than I had been of my movements.

"They loved it," Layla said. "No thanks to you."

I had been trying to find a way to hold my arms casually away from my body, hoping to discourage the sweat from soaking through my shirt. But now I crossed them over my chest defensively.

"What do you mean?" I asked. "I did the full twist in the layout position, like we talked about."

Even though it was just a full twist, I was kind of sorry that Mo hadn't been able to see it. Twists were not generally my forte, but I thought the two I'd done today out on that basketball court had been really tight, especially given that I wasn't getting the usual bounce from the floor mat.

"Yeah, and then we talked about a *double* twist," Layla pointed out. "Remember? If you're not going to come up big, why do it at all?"

As far as I knew, Layla could do a cartwheel, a back walkover, and splits, and that was it. So I took a deep breath and tried to explain it to her. It was possible that she wasn't meaning to be a jerk, but just didn't have the gymnastics background to understand what she was asking of me.

"In a cheer competition with the mats, I could do it," I said. "No problem. But on the basketball court . . . the impact could really hurt my ankles, or worse, if I don't land it. It's hard to get the height I need on the wood floors."

"So, lose some weight," Layla said, "and maybe you could fly higher."

I stared at her, stunned. Was that a personal dig, or a general comment? I hadn't told her about my therapy, but I couldn't help being paranoid. "This is muscle weight," I said, repeating the words I'd heard from the nutritionist Mo had hired. She came to talk to us once a month, giving us recipes and meal plans for how to keep ourselves healthy. "I can't *lose* weight—I'm already in really good shape."

It was weird. I felt like I'd heard other people say those words a thousand times—Mo, Britt, my mother, my therapist—but I'd never felt one hundred percent like *I* believed them until now, standing there defending myself against Layla.

Layla shrugged, as if she was already over this conversation, and turned around to chat with Stephenie and Ashley. I heard them talking about their tosses, Layla claiming that she could almost touch the ceiling of the gym, that was how high she'd gotten. I didn't need Norman's math skills to know that that was impossible and was intended to be a dig at me.

I thought back to the photo-booth pictures I'd taken with Layla, at the way she'd directed the whole thing so easily. Smile, be silly, now give your best fierce face. It was almost like she'd done it a bunch of times before, and I was starting to think that "friends forever" really meant friends for as long as it suited her.

I glanced up at the clock on the wall. The pep rally wasn't supposed to be over for another fifteen minutes, but I bet if I called Mo, she'd pick me up on her way to the frozen yogurt place in time for me to do some serious team-building.

Fourteen

Britt, Christina, and Noelle all looked surprised to see me when I ordered my usual fat-free white chocolate frozen yogurt and sat down with them at the booth.

"Love your outfit," Britt said sarcastically.

I glanced down at myself. I'd forgotten I was still wearing my cheerleading uniform, which was blue, with BHS in big white letters going diagonally across the chest. Instead of the classic pleated skirt I'd always associated with cheerleading, we wore straight skirts with a little slit in the thigh. I'd been excited to change into my uniform after gym that morning, and it was kind of cool to walk around school all day wearing something that so clearly declared me part of a group. But now, I felt silly.

"It's not all it's cracked up to be," I said, and smiled through a spoonful of white chocolate yogurt.

Britt looked at me skeptically. "Just like that?" she said. "You're back?"

"Oh, give her a break," Christina said. "I'm actually kind of curious about cheerleading. Is it like in all the movies?"

I spent the next twenty minutes describing the practices, which, looking back on it, hadn't been all that fun. Even gymnastics workouts, which were way more intense and left my muscles aching sometimes for days afterward, were better. At least I felt like I was challenging myself, and surrounding myself with people who cared about me and were interesting to talk to.

"Listen," Britt said, cutting in at a random point. Everyone got quiet. It was clear from the tone of her voice that she had something to say other than a comment on pom-poms. "If you ever don't want to be my—*our*—friend, then fine. Just say so, okay?"

"Believe me," I said, "I want to hang out with you guys. I'm sorry I ditched you on Halloween;

that was really stupid. I had such an awful time that night."

"I liked your dress, though," Christina said, waggling her eyebrows. "I'm going to borrow it if I actually go on a real date. Maybe with Mihai?"

Noelle made a show of plugging her ears. "Seriously!" she said. "Not funny."

"That reminds me," I said to Britt, partially to prevent Noelle's head from exploding. "Remember that guy Norman? I think you guys would really hit it off. I kind of messed up with him, too, but if I ever convince him to talk to me again, maybe I can set you up in time for the eighth grade dance."

Britt rolled her eyes. "Uh, I think you're forgetting a couple of things," she said. "Number one, boys have cooties. Number two, we're Elite gymnasts. We should be dreaming about dismounts and deductions, rather than dating and dances."

I glanced at Noelle, who was suddenly very focused on her mango sorbet. I knew she was thinking about David, the boy who'd kissed her last year at the dance. Even though they were only friends—Noelle was way too serious about her gymnastics to let a boy interfere with that—she still blushed if anyone mentioned his name.

Normally, this would have been about the time I started feeling very self-conscious about the fact that the other three girls *were* Elite gymnasts, whereas I wasn't. But for some reason, it didn't bother me this time. The Elite qualifier was coming up, and I allowed myself to really think about it for the first time in a while. My vault was strong, and my bar and beam routines were both fairly solid. If I could only work on that one tumbling pass, I knew I could qualify.

"Speaking of being Elite," I said, now that I could say the word without feeling a knot forming in my stomach, "do you guys know what you're going to do about that stipend from USAG?"

Noelle and Christina glanced at each other. "I'm taking it," Noelle said. "I know it means that I can't compete in college, and I'm sad about that. But my family could really use the help with all the training costs, so I think it's the best thing to do."

I knew that it wasn't easy for her parents to pay for all the leotards and equipment and travel costs and weekly gym fees; the summer before, we'd held a car wash for Noelle, to raise money for her to go to the Junior National Championships.

"I'm not going to take it," Christina said, and although she left it at that, I was able to fill in the rest. Her dad was a big-deal cardiologist who traveled all the time to speak at conferences, and they had a ton of money, so I knew that that wasn't a concern for her.

I couldn't even begin to think what I would have done in that situation. Although I'd have loved to compete in the Olympics, I wasn't honestly sure if that was ever going to happen, so I thought it'd be nice to keep the option of college open. But it was my parents' money, so I felt like it would be their decision at the end of the day.

By *parents*, of course, I meant my mother and Rick, my stepfather. I rarely let myself think about my dad these days. I was still upset that he'd stood me up again, but I was more depressed at how inevitable it had felt. He never came through when he said he would. Even when he came to the parade, he'd come as a reporter with an idea for a human-interest story, not as a dad who cared about his daughter. I guess I had to give him credit for leaving a message on my cell phone the day after my birthday and apologizing for missing dinner, but I'd never called him back, and he hadn't left any other messages. He probably thought it was all settled. He'd apologized so I wouldn't be mad anymore or hold it against him.

But I hadn't really forgiven him. I'd just given up.

I realized I'd been sitting there staring off into space, and so I forced myself to smile and get back to enjoying my friends. "You'll make the Olympics, Noelle," I said. "I know it. They were even talking about you on the broadcast for that USA vs. the World meet, saying that you were someone to watch."

Noelle flushed. "Thanks," she said. "It was so much fun. People started clapping when I did my beam mount, even though there was a senior girl competing on the bars at the same time."

"I bet that threw her off," I said. Not that I wanted any other gymnast to fall or mess up, but there was something exciting about knowing that one of my friends could take attention away from a girl who might compete in the Olympics next year.

Gymnastics is a funny sport in that, ultimately, you're alone up there on the balance beam, which makes it easy sometimes to feel completely separated from other people. But as Britt grinned at me across the table, I realized that being part of a team also meant more than just wearing matching ribbons in your hair and striking the same pose. It meant having people who cared about you, and who would do anything in their power to boost you up, rather than tear you down.

Mo dropped me off at my house after our frozen yogurt outing, and I practically threw my backpack down in the foyer as I came in. My cheerleading uniform was starting to feel like a hot, itchy straitjacket, and I couldn't wait to get out of it.

In the kitchen, I ran into Tiffany. She was pulling a Pop-Tart from the toaster, holding it the way she held things when she had painted her nails and she didn't want to touch anything while they were still wet.

"Those were some pretty sick moves," she said. It took me a second to realize that she was talking to me, and that she was referring to the pep rally. She'd been performing at the pep rally, too, as a flag girl, but it hadn't occurred to me to stay and watch her. This would have made me feel like a terrible stepsister, except that Tiffany had never shown any interest in anything I'd done before.

"Thanks," I said uncertainly, and then I was compelled to add, "I didn't do the double twist."

She didn't respond. I was about to head to my room when she finally spoke. "At least you didn't lose your balance on the most basic pyramid ever," Tiffany said. "I wouldn't worry about your double twist until they can finish a routine without crashing and burning."

Apparently I'd really been in my own world during the whole routine, because I didn't remember anyone falling. I couldn't believe I'd missed that. It had to have been one of the flyers, which meant that it was Layla or Stephenie or Ashley.

"Cute uniform, though," Tiffany commented, raking her eyes over the miniskirt and top. She was still in her sparkly flag-girl costume, which consisted of a halter top and tight, shiny pants. I'd seen a bunch of other flag girls around school that day wearing the same thing.

Of course. *That* was why Tiffany was talking to me now. These were her people, the cheerleaders and flag girls and homecoming queens. As much as I was enjoying this bonus attention from her, I felt like I had to set the record straight. "I'm quitting cheerleading," I said.

"Oh, thank God," Tiffany said. It was so not the response that I'd been expecting that for a second I just stared at her.

"Thanks a lot," I said, stiffening. So I didn't fit the usual stereotype of a cheerleader or belong to that crowd. She didn't have to rub my nose in it.

She rolled her eyes, licking strawberry filling off her index finger. "Come on," she said. "JV is a joke. Everyone knows that."

"They're not a—" I started defending the cheerleading squad automatically, then stopped myself. "Wait. What do you mean?"

"I was a cheerleader when I was nine and we did more stuff," she said. "The two good people who were in JV last year moved up to varsity, and now it's a bunch of newbies and wannabes and Ms. Hinnen, who has no idea what she's doing."

"She seems like she does," I said, but I realized that I'd only heard her yell a lot. At the gym, Mo and Cheng hardly said a word, but then, they didn't have to. They could look at you and you knew whether they were proud of you or believed that you could do better.

"Well, I don't hang out with freshmen"— Tiffany said the word like she might have said *dirty underwear*—"but I can tell you that Layla and her crowd shouldn't be dusting their shelves for that state trophy any time soon. Our JV is probably the worst in the county."

I remembered the horribly stupid cheer I'd done for tryouts and wanted to hide my flaming face, in case Tiffany somehow guessed what an idiot I'd been that day. "No wonder they picked me," I said.

"Oh, they didn't pick you because you're *bad*," Tiffany said. "They picked you because you can tumble, and they needed *someone* on that team who can do *something*."

I thought back on all the practices, and the pep rally, where all I'd done was flip from one side to another and back again like a performing monkey.

"So, yeah," Tiffany said. "Good job on quitting."

I smiled. "Now I guess you think I should be a flag girl, huh?" I said.

"Absolutely not," she said, making a face.

I'd been joking, but I was a little stung by Tiffany's response, even though I guess I should've expected it. She'd probably have been embarrassed to have me around, and would have tried to convince the team that we didn't know each other at all. Just because she was being nice to me this one time didn't mean that she'd want me to be a part of the flag corps.

"I was kidding," I said. "It's your thing; I get it."

"Yeah," she said. "It's what I do because it's kind of fun and I hang out with my friends and stuff. But you're, like, an awesome gymnast, who competes all over the state and gets to be on the news. If I could do even half of what you can, I'd quit the flag corps tomorrow."

I didn't know what to say. It was easily the nicest— and longest—thing Tiffany had ever said to me.

"Although you guys don't get boobs, right?" Tiffany added. "That might be a little weird. I don't know if I would trade that part."

I thought of that ridiculous little bra with the pink bow, the one that Layla had made fun of before I knew her name, and the one I hadn't even worn yet. And then, I couldn't help it: I started laughing. Tiffany looked at me like I was crazy, but eventually she let out a chuckle in spite of herself.

"All that flipping has made the blood rush to your head," she said. "You're nuts." But for the first time in a while, I felt like everything was actually very clear. I knew what I wanted, and I knew what I had to do.

Fifteen

I knew they were holding Saturday cheerleading practice at the school, even though I usually missed Saturdays, to work out at the gym instead. This time, I made an exception. Mo wasn't thrilled about my losing an hour of training, but she seemed somewhat mollified when she found out the reason behind it.

"So, you done with that," she said. "No more cheer?"

"No more cheer," I assured her firmly.

"Good," she said, nodding her head. "You have Elite qualifier in very short time, and we need to get you ready."

"Believe me," I said. "I'm ready."

My mom wasn't superexcited about carting me from the gym to school and back again on her Saturday morning, either, but I was surprised to find that she seemed pretty pleased about my reason, too.

"I thought you liked that I was a cheerleader," I said.

She paused, as if thinking carefully about what to say next. "I was happy to see that you had some friends at school," she said, "although I wasn't sure if they seemed like the nicest girls. And of course, if you decided that you wanted to be a cheerleader instead of devoting yourself to gymnastics, that would be okay. I know gymnastics is a big commitment, and you're getting to be a young woman. You may decide there are other things you want in life."

Oh, no. Not the "young woman" speech. My mom was on the brink of another teary memory about how much I'd grown; my goal was to head it off at the pass.

She was too quick for me, though. "What did you say that song was, that you danced around the living room to?"

"'Abracadabra,'" I said, hoping that we wouldn't have to dig out old home videos that night.

"That was it." My mom smiled, remembering. "You've always loved gymnastics. But if that changes down the road, well, that's part of growing up."

I'd gotten started in the sport when my mom told me that we were going to the mall to take pictures, and that I should wear a leotard, to pretend that I was a gymnast in the picture. I'd gotten a gymnastics Barbie doll for Christmas once and thought gymnasts were awesome. But when she stopped the car, we weren't at the mall. Instead, we were at Texas Twisters, and I was taking my first tumbling class. They'd let me jump on a trampoline and fall into a pit of foam, and I'd never looked back.

Then, somewhere in the last few years, gymnastics had started to get really hard, and not as much fun. I guess I had thought that it was as simple as snapping my fingers and then poof! Everything would happen like magic. But my body was a little thicker than the other girls', my hips a little wider, and the moves didn't come as easily. I started thinking that maybe it wasn't worth it, that maybe I should give it all up.

Even in the past few months, though, I'd really

missed it. I missed my teammates and my coaches. I missed the exhilaration of doing a skill that only a handful of people in the world could do and working on it until it was as close to perfect as possible. I missed the challenge of gymnastics, which was so much more than flipping across a floor and then turning around and doing it again.

"Wish me luck," I said to my mom when we pulled up in front of the school.

She leaned over and pressed her lips to my cheek in a kiss. "You don't need it," she said.

Layla, Stephenie, and Ashley were standing around at the sidelines of the football field, their hands on their hips, surveying the girls who usually formed the base in our routines, who were doing sit-ups. "Are you tired already?" Layla snarked at one girl. "Maybe that's why you drop me all the time— because you have the stamina of my eighty-five-year-old grandmother."

"Hello," I said.

Layla spun to look at me.

"Nice of you to make a practice for once," she said. "What's that?"

I had been holding my folded uniform, and

now I passed it to her. "I quit," I said simply.

"You *quit*?" she repeated, and everyone stopped. The girls on the grass froze in mid-sit-up, and Stephenie and Ashley glanced at each other and then back at me.

"I have a big qualifier coming up, and I need to prepare for it," I said, reciting the canned excuse I'd rehearsed in the mirror that morning. Of course, that wasn't the only reason, but I figured there was no need to rehash everything. I would be professional about it all, and grown-up.

"You can't just *quit*," Layla said, her mouth twisting over the word. "We need you."

I thought about what Tiffany had said, and I wanted to say, *I know*, but I held my tongue. Still, I couldn't resist a pointed "Maybe you'll find someone who can do your double twist that you want so much."

Framed by her blond hair, Layla's face burned red, as though she knew exactly what I was calling her on. "Fine," she said. "But if you leave, there's no coming back. You can change your mind, but we won't change ours. You're out."

"Okay," I said. "Well, see ya." I waved at Stephenie and Ashley, to let them know I was including them in that farewell, before starting back to my mom's car.

"Wait," Layla called after me, and I turned around. "I was going to tell you . . ." She glanced nervously at Stephenie and Ashley, before giving a defiant toss of her head. "My dad lets me take two friends to New York City every Christmas. He rents a penthouse right on Central Park. I was thinking about taking you this year, if you were on JV with me."

Ashley's eyebrows drew together, and Stephenie started forward.

"Wait a minute—" Layla said, but I shook my head.

"I don't want to go to Central Park with you," I said. "I have friends already. You met them at my birthday party."

"Oh, *those* losers," Layla sneered. "I wouldn't brag about it."

I ignored this, walking backward so I could still see her as I moved toward the car. "And Norman!" I added. "Norman's my friend, too."

"Well!" Layla said, and I could tell that she was trying to formulate an insult, but coming up empty.

I was just glad to get that cheerleading uniform

off my back. It was no wonder it had felt like a straitjacket—it had been restraining me from pursuing everything that really mattered.

The next day, I looked Norman up in the school directory. It turned out that he didn't live too far from me, so I borrowed my stepbrother's bike, which was way too big for me, and which he would definitely *not* have wanted me riding, and showed up on Norman's doorstep.

Norman opened the door wearing a T-shirt that read, IT'S ALL RELATIVE, EINSTEIN, and his crooked glasses. "Hello, Jessie," he said, as though it wasn't that random for me to be there.

"I wanted to tell you that I'm sorry," I blurted out. "Please don't think that I'm a cheater. It's only that I've been doing really terrible in Mr. Freeman's class, and I'm used to getting As, but then I realized that was because a lot of my teachers are pretty understanding about my gymnastics schedule, except that Mr. Freeman said I shouldn't expect a free ride, and it's not that I want special treatment or anything, but—"

Norman opened the door wider and gestured for me to come into the house, cutting off my rambling. "I was studying for the test," he said, "if you want to do flash cards with me."

I smiled. "I would love to."

Unfortunately, it wasn't as easy to work on the double front tuck that was giving me problems. I knew what I had to do—right now, my body was pitched too far back when I came out of my front handspring, so I couldn't get the height on the double tuck—but gymnastics was different from school. It wasn't enough for you to know something with your mind; you had to know it with your whole body.

I landed on my heels again, and then my butt was on the floor. At least we still had extra mats at one corner of the floor, providing a little relief on those hard landings. Cheng made the time-out signal, as if he wanted to stop a nonexistent clock, and crossed over to me.

"You need to do in pit?" he asked. The foam pit was where we usually tried new skills first, so that we could practice them over and over without risking our bodies. I remembered when I'd first started at Texas Twisters, I'd looked forward to any time I could play in the pit, even if it was just jumping down the runway like a pogo stick and then flinging myself into the soft squares of foam at the end. We trained in the pit all the time toward actual goals, but it still felt like playing.

But now, it felt almost like an insult, as if Cheng was saying I couldn't do the skill. I shook my head, but he was already leading me to the pit. "Come," he said, gesturing to an assistant coach to take over on floor where he'd left off.

There were younger girls using the pit, but Cheng asked them to take a break. I might not technically have been an Elite yet, but this was one of the ways I knew I had reached the top at this gym. Mo and Cheng gave the four of us a lot more attention than they gave to the lower-level gymnasts, and if we needed equipment, we always had first dibs. At one point, I'd been the girl being asked to move. This time, I was the girl that others were moving for.

There was something kind of cool about that, but I also didn't want the younger girls to think that I was so bad that I couldn't even get this tumbling pass without extra help. A double front tuck was an E skill in the code of points, which USA Gymnastics updated every few years to reflect the number of points you could get for a skill in a routine. A single tucked flip would be an A skill, and the code of points went all the way up to G, which meant that an E skill was on the hard side, but not the hardest. I felt like I should have been able to do it by now.

Once the younger girls had moved off to work on the trampoline, Cheng made a sweeping gesture toward the pit. "Go," he said.

I ran up the length of floor, throwing my body into a front handspring, and then curled my body up for the double tuck. I landed in the pit, cradled by the foam squares, and yet I didn't feel comforted. If we'd been on the floor, I would've ended up on my butt for the thousandth time. It might have been a different venue, but I was getting the same results.

I climbed out of the pit, feeling dejected, but Cheng stopped me, clasping my shoulders. "You need to commit," he said, and then let go, indicating that I should do it again.

I wanted to ask him what he meant by that. Commit to *what*? What was I not committing to? But with Cheng, four words was already a speech, and you couldn't count on getting any more out of him.

I took my place at the end of the strip of floor, flexing my toes by curling them under and pressing them on the carpet. I ran forward, leapt into my front handspring, and then tucked my body for the double flip, but I knew I was short.

"Commit," Cheng repeated, and I set up to go again, even though I still didn't know exactly what he meant.

We did this three more times before I got frustrated. I felt like the gymnastics equivalent of a broken record. Why would he make me do this over and over without *telling* me what I was doing wrong? It seemed pointless. The Elite qualifier was that weekend, and so far I had a twenty-five percent chance of landing on my butt for this skill, and a one hundred percent chance that I'd get at least a couple of tenths deducted for that.

But Cheng twirled his finger, telling me *again*. So I got set again, squaring my shoulders and standing very straight, like there was a steel rod where my spine should have been. If he wanted me to waste my entire morning practice doing this one thing, then, fine. Meanwhile, the other girls were perfecting their dance moves on the floor, but I was stuck in a loop, running into a foam pit.

This time, when I launched into my front handspring, I was kind of angry, and so I pushed the floor with my hands, as if I were pushing someone away.

My feet pounded the springy mat, making a satisfying *thunk*, and then I felt my body lifting almost on its own, curling instinctively into a tight little ball and doing two rotations in the air before I floated down into the pit.

That was what was weird. I'd started out so mad, but by the time I was done with the double tuck, it was like all that fury had gone away, leaving me feeling light and calm. My body weighed nothing, suspended in midair until I came down feetfirst, straight as an arrow, into the center of the pit.

"Yes!" Cheng shouted, and I realized I was still standing, surrounded by foam squares. I'd landed it perfectly! If I had been on the floor, I would've *drilled* it.

"How'd I do that?" I asked, but I didn't really need an answer. I'd felt the strong, decisive movements in my body, almost like I was fighting with the floor. But in the end, it had been the floor that helped me, giving me the lift I needed and propelling me through two flawless tucked flips. I'd committed to my gymnastics, and I felt like I had gotten commitment back.

Sixteen

"**Y**ou seem to have figured out a lot since the last time I saw you," Dr. Fisher said at our next session. I had just finished telling her about quitting the cheerleading squad, landing my double front, and taking my American Government test, which I thought I'd done really well on. I even felt good about the question on the necessary and proper clause, thanks to Norman and his flash cards.

"Yeah," I said. "It's been a crazy week."

Dr. Fisher's mouth curled up slightly at the edges. I wondered if that was a therapist's way of saying, *I told you so*. She was the one, after all, who'd basically challenged me to figure out what I wanted, rather than focusing on what I thought other people wanted for me or for themselves.

Maybe that was why Dr. Fisher didn't ask many questions. She knew the answers, but she wanted me to find those answers for myself.

There was one question, though, that I'd been wondering about for a while, and I still didn't have any closure on. "Why don't we talk more about my eating?" I asked.

"You want to talk about your eating," she repeated.

"Yes," I said. "I mean, no. I don't know—but it's why I'm here, isn't it? I was trying to lose weight, and so I wasn't eating. We discussed it sometimes when I first started coming here, but lately it's like we don't ever mention it. Does that mean I'm cured?"

Dr. Fisher leaned back in her chair, looking at me from behind those funky glasses. "Do you feel like you're cured?"

Wasn't that what *she* was supposed to tell *me*? I wasn't the doctor. Obviously, I hadn't been able to diagnose myself in the first place, so I was hardly going to be able to declare myself cured.

"I don't know," I said. "You haven't said so,

and I'm still coming here, so I guess not."

Dr. Fisher set her notebook down on the table, and I tried to crane my neck to see what was written on it. I wondered if it was stuff I'd said or her ideas about me. Maybe she just doodled on the thing during our sessions, pretending she was listening when really she was thinking about her grocery list.

"We don't talk about it because I don't want you to feel confined by words like *cured*," Dr. Fisher said. "It's not about a label that says you're magically better. Getting better is a process. Does that make sense?"

"So, then, why don't we talk about my eating?" I said. "I still freak out about the way I look in a leotard sometimes, or how much I weigh before a big competition. It's hard for me not to think about how many calories are in a slice of birthday cake, even though I'll eat it."

"And that's a normal part of the process," Dr. Fisher said. "Mo hired a nutritionist to talk to you girls about your health, is that right?"

For the past several months, our nutritionist had visited the gym regularly and shown us charts about food groups and the anatomy of the human body, discussing the fuel that we need from food and the best way to keep our bodies running efficiently. She even gave us recipes to take home, including one for a fruit smoothie with protein powder that my mom had started making for me as a treat.

"I know that with the help of that nutritionist, you're working on your eating behaviors," Dr. Fisher said. "Of course, I'm always open to talk about that, too. You lead these sessions, Jessie, not me."

I tried to think back on things we'd discussed in the past, and realized that she was right. Usually, I'd brought up the topic of conversation in some way or other, whether at the beginning of our sessions or in response to something she'd said. "But if I'm not talking about food," I said, "you might think I was trying to hide something, right?"

Dr. Fisher pursed her lips, moving her head back and forth like she was considering two options. "Not necessarily," she said. "It's not about the food, really. It's about whatever else is going on in your life that makes you unhappy, or stressed, or angry. So, if that's what you want to bring here to me, then that's what I want to help you with."

When I remembered my worst times—for instance, right around when Britt had started at Texas Twisters and I'd been consumed with practicing for my first Elite qualifier, the one I'd never gotten to compete at—it was true that I'd been feeling a lot of those emotions. Like, right now, I felt immense pressure about the upcoming qualifier, even though I knew I was ready. I felt anxiety over Mr. Freeman's class, even though I thought I'd rocked the test. But I also felt hopeful about the future, and excited about gymnastics and school and my friends, both old and new.

"There is one thing I want to talk about," I said.

Dr. Fisher picked her notebook back up. "Anything," she said, smiling.

I realized that I'd often thought her smiles were smug or insincere or patronizing; but this one really didn't seem that way. It looked nice, like she was interested, and open to whatever I had to say.

"You know my parents are divorced," I said. "And my dad lives in Austin, only half an hour away from us, yet I only see him a few times a year. . . ."

I filled Dr. Fisher in on everything that I'd never told her before, about how he sent cards always before or after my birthday, but never *on* it, about how he'd say he'd be somewhere and then cancel or never show up, about how he didn't like me coming to his apartment because, he said, I'd be "bored" there, about the time he called me on my cell phone randomly and I was so happy because he barely ever called, but then it turned out he'd pocket-dialed me and I heard him laughing with someone at lunch.

Talking felt a lot like the reps that Mo made us do, where we strapped weights around our ankles and practiced our leaps. While the weights were on, my calf muscles would burn and my thighs would feel like lead, as though they couldn't possibly extend any further or do any more work. But once the weights were off, that was when I could finally fly.

It turned out that I got an eighty-eight on my American Government midterm. Not as great as Norman, who got a 105 for answering everything correctly *and* getting a bonus question right, but still a lot better than the sixty-seven I had gotten before. Mr. Freeman even pulled me aside after class to congratulate me, and it felt nice to be singled out for a *good* reason for once.

"Mr. Freeman?" I said before I left.

He was shuffling papers at his desk, tapping them against the surface until all the edges lined up. "Yes?"

I cleared my throat. "I just wanted to say that

I was paying attention. Before, when I said that I believed that the end justified the means, I wasn't really thinking about it. But now I get why there are checks and balances to make sure no one goes too far."

I hoped he figured that I was talking about our government, and not about myself. Even though I was kind of talking about both. Of course, I understood why no branch of the government should have absolute power, but I also felt like it was a good thing to keep in mind in life, too. My friends kept me in check about my gymnastics, my therapist kept me in check about my health, Norman kept me in check about my schoolwork. So did Mr. Freeman, and I wanted him to know that I appreciated it.

"I'm sorry if I was hard on you," he said. "But, like I said, I know about being an athlete, and I know that an athlete always strives for excellence. You have a competition coming up, isn't that right?"

There had been a little article about it in the sports section of the newspaper, which I knew Mr. Freeman read at his desk while we did our classwork from the board. "Yes, sir."

I thought for a moment that he was going to remind me not to slack off on my studies, but he just smiled. "Then you know what you have to do, right?"

I shook my head.

He winked at me. "Be excellent."

The day of the Elite qualifier, my stomach was in knots and I kept playing with the clips in my hair, snapping and unsnapping them in an attempt to burn off the restless energy coursing through my body. I was waiting to compete on my first event—vault—when Mo stopped me and took my hands, looking me right in the eye.

"You will do this," she said.

And I didn't have time to doubt her, because the judges were holding up the green flag, letting me know that it was my turn to go. Mo gave me a pat on the small of my back, and then she stepped away, leaving me alone at the end of the vault runway.

I sprinted toward the vaulting table, throwing my body into a round-off onto the springboard, then adding a half twist so I was facing forward as my hands hit the vault. My vault was a front pike with another half twist, and I bent my knees slightly to absorb the shock of the landing. I'd stuck it!

"That's it," Mo said, hugging my shoulder as I climbed back into my warm-up suit and waited for the score. When it flashed, it was one of the highest I'd ever gotten on vault in a competition, and I knew that I was well on my way toward qualifying for the Elite team.

Mo and Cheng always cautioned us against paying too much attention to our scores or to other competitors, worrying that we'd get distracted, or complacent, or anxious, and that that would affect our performances. But the truth of the matter is that it was hard not to think about those things. Math was one of my worst subjects, and still I was able to figure out this equation fairly easily. My high vault score meant that I had a little bit of wiggle room, but I still had my hardest events coming up, so I couldn't breathe freely just yet.

The uneven bars was not my favorite event. Noelle was very efficient on them, as she was on everything else—she would mount the bars, get the job done with straight legs, pointed toes, and knees together, and then stick her landing and move on. Christina had a slow, easy rhythm to her bar work; her routine wasn't the most difficult of all of ours, but her pirouettes and stalder skills fit her long lines and graceful body. For Britt, the uneven bars were one gigantic playground—she loved to try daring moves, swinging fast and flipping high. Right now, she was trying to learn a Comaneci on the bars; this was a superdifficult release skill that she crashed on more than she actually succeeded in. That might have been enough to discourage me from putting it in my routine, but Britt saw it as a challenge.

Sometimes, just getting from one bar to another felt like a challenge to me. During practice, I often had more difficulty with my uphill transition from the low bar to the high bar than I did with my release skill—which was weird, because technically, the release skill was a harder move, with a higher point value.

So, once I mounted the bar and started my routine, I allowed myself a single second of relief after I made it through that transition, where I touched my toes on the bar, my body completely piked as I circled the low bar once and jumped to the high bar. But then I was swinging all the way around the high bar, letting go at the top to spin and catch it again.

That was how it was on bars: there was no time to think, no time to question. My momentum kept me going, and I didn't stop until my feet touched the mat. I took one step back, which would cost me a couple of tenths at the most, but my hands had grabbed the bar when they were supposed to and let go when they were supposed to, and I was done with two of my events.

We moved on to beam, where I had to wait before my chance to compete. It took a while for each gymnast to go, and then it was easily the most nerve-racking of all of the events, so every minute on the sidelines felt like an hour. I did stretches to keep my muscles warm, lifting one leg at my side until my calf nearly touched my ear, and using a line in the carpet to work on my sheep jump. In a sheep jump, you throw your head back and touch your toes to the back of your head, so the landing is completely blind. Not only is it blind, but your equilibrium is off a little, as though you had just gone on the spinning teacups ride at the fair and now you were trying to stay balanced on a four-inch-wide surface. I did a couple of reps of the jump on the floor, and each time, my feet landed squarely on the line in the carpet.

Although I couldn't stop myself from check-ing out my scores and taking notice when another competitor got a loud cheer or a gasp, I had been trying to avoid searching the crowd for my family and friends. I knew that they were all there—my mom, Rick, Tiffany, and my three teammates. I even knew where they were sitting; after all, this wasn't the USA vs. the World event. It was just a local qualifier, where girls of various levels were competing to move up to the next one, and so the crowd was decent but not huge.

Plus, Rick had worn his favorite orange hunting cap, which I could see as a bright spot out of the corner of my eye. The funny thing was that he didn't even hunt.

My dad had called at the last minute and asked if I wanted him to be at the competition. That was exactly how he phrased it, too—not that he would like to be there, or that he was looking forward to it, but almost checking to see if I absolutely *needed* him there. I told him no, I didn't, and he seemed relieved. I wasn't sure if I was ready to confront him yet, but I was definitely ready to stop expecting him to be something he wasn't—a real dad. He congratulated me and said he was proud of me, and I said thank you and pretended I thought he meant it.

"Jessie," Mo said, reminding me that I had more pressing things to be worrying about just then. "You go."

I knew right from my mount that I was a little off. Sometimes you just felt that kind of thing, even before you went into the rest of your routine. The springboard would feel a bit weird or you'd land a little crooked or you'd have butterflies in your stomach that wouldn't calm down . . . whatever it was, the worst thing you could do was dwell on it. So, even though my mind was racing—*you almost missed a foot on the beam; that could've been catastrophic; you're lucky to even be on*—I tried to take a deep breath before my acrobatic series.

Usually, if a gymnast falls on anything, it's the acrobatic series across the beam. It can be super-tricky to time everything right, and if you get off by even a fraction of an inch on one skill, it can create a domino effect. If you're only doing a single flip, then you might wobble but you won't fall. But if you're trying to do one flip after the other, a minor error on the first could make your second disastrous.

These were all of the things I was trying *not* to think about as I lined my feet up on the beam and held my arms up straight by my ears. Then I threw myself into a back handspring into another back handspring into a back layout, landing with both of my feet on the beam at once. This was an important part of the skill, because it gave it extra difficulty. If I failed to keep my body pencil straight the entire time, I lost a couple of tenths of a point, and I risked bobbling or falling off the beam entirely.

This time, I didn't do it perfectly. I could feel that my hips and body weren't aligned, so I piked the landing a bit, but I was able to get upright fast enough that the judges might not have noticed. I was so relieved to be through that part of the routine that I almost felt like it was over.

But then came my sheep jump. I'd practiced it so many times that I wasn't worried about it. I bounced on the balls of my feet, trying to get the height that I needed, and threw my head back. When I was in the air, I could feel the tips of my toes brush my ponytail, sending strands of hair swinging around my face.

When I landed, my feet were not square on the beam. One was almost completely off, and I curled my toes around the beam as if I could somehow hold myself on with the same move that I would have used to pick up a towel from the floor when I didn't want to bend over.

Somehow, it worked. I wobbled quite a bit—that would be at least three tenths of a point, probably more—but I stayed on the beam. It could've been a lot worse, though it was hard to view it as a victory.

I could feel tears stinging my eyes as I dismounted and found Mo's arms, which were ready to be wrapped around me. "Okay," she said. "Okay."

There were a lot of ways I could have interpreted that word: that my routine had been fine, not great but not awful; that I was going to be okay. But the only thing I wanted to find out was whether my score would be enough to keep me in the running to qualify as an Elite gymnast.

Now I couldn't stop myself from finding my mother in the crowd. I sought out the bright orange hat and saw her, one hand over her mouth. As soon as she saw me; she waved and tried to smile, but I could tell she was worried. I glanced away before I totally psyched myself out.

I had to move to floor for my final event. Normally, floor was an event I liked and that I was good at. I'd even been feeling confident about the double front that had been causing me problems before. But now, I wasn't so sure. I didn't know what I needed to score in order to qualify as Elite, or even if it was possible.

As if reading my mind, Mo stood in front of me, commanding my attention with her gaze. Back in China, Mo had been an Elite gymnast herself, so you could still see that competitive fire burning in her eyes.

"You can do this," she said. "You work hard for long time. You deserve this."

At first, I wanted to correct her—I felt like I hadn't been working as hard as I should have been lately. I was taking time off for my treatment, of course, and then I lost precious hours to the earlier start at the high school and the cheerleading practices I'd been attending. Maybe if I hadn't wasted that time, I could've had more reps on my sheep jump, and maybe then I wouldn't have faltered here, when the stakes were so high.

But I'd also been in the gym six days a week, often six hours a day, for the past three years. Before that, I'd trained with the team and traveled to competitions most weekends, performing at invitationals and qualifiers and exhibitions.

I glanced up at the crowd, seeking out my teammates, the girls who had been with me every step of the way. Britt nudged Christina, and Christina tapped Noelle, and then the three of them stood up, holding signs. Britt's sign was upside down at first, but she turned it right side up, laughing, and I saw that, together, the three signs read GO JESSIE GO! in huge letters.

I couldn't stop a grin from spreading across my face. Sometimes I got jealous about the fact that they were already Elite gymnasts and had the opportunity to participate in all of these amazing competitions, like the Nationals and the USA vs. the World event. But this was my meet today, and it was my chance to prove to everyone—and to myself—that I *could* do it.

I was still smiling when I struck my beginning pose on the floor. There was a small chime that let me know my music was about to begin, and as soon as I heard the first note, I danced my way to one corner of the blue carpet.

Although I'd been struggling with the double front, I had a longer tumbling pass that took up more of my energy, and so we'd put that one right at the start of the routine. Generally, it's a good idea to begin with your most difficult pass, so that you are fresh and not too tired to get through your hardest skill. So I launched into my first pass, which consisted of a round-off to a couple of whip backs to a double twist in a layout position, and then tried to catch my breath before I had to do my next one.

Normally, as I stood surveying the blue carpet in front of me as if it were an expanse of ocean I was about to flip across, I was completely in the zone. I heard my music almost in a vacuum, and it wasn't uncommon for me to finish the routine feeling like the whole thing had happened in a blur. But this time, as I set up my second tumbling pass, I became very aware of the crowd. I heard a voice—Britt's piercing yell: "Go, Jessie, go!" Then more voices joined in: Noelle and Christina and my mom, and it sounded like the entire crowd was chanting my name, even though I knew that that was probably not even possible. But it lifted me up, and reminded me of that day with Cheng when I'd attacked the tumbling pass into the pit. Maybe now, like then, I would fly.

I sprinted across the floor, jumping into my front handspring and then pushing off with my feet to rotate quickly two times in the air. My feet hit the floor, and I didn't even take a little step back the way I normally did, dancing the landing a little bit to make it look more solid than it was. I left my feet right where they were—firmly on the ground.

The audience cheered when I finished my routine, all four tumbling passes and my dance elements. I walked sedately off the floor in the elegant way that the judges like to see, with my arms straight at my sides and my head held high, but I couldn't help almost running as I threw myself into Mo's arms for a hug.

I didn't even have to look at the scoreboard this time—I just knew I'd qualified to be an Elite gymnast. I was done flipping between two worlds, feeling like I didn't fit into either. Now, I had one place where I knew I would always belong.

Gymnastics Glossary

all-around competition: The part of a competition where gymnasts compete in all four events, and in which their combined scores are used to determine who is the best all-around athlete

basket toss: A stunt that involves three or more cheerleaders who interlock their arms to form a base for another, who takes a standing position on this base and is then thrown by yet another cheerleader into the air to perform a jump, before returning to the "cradle" of the bases' hands

beam: A horizontal, raised apparatus that is four inches wide, sixteen feet in length, and approximately four feet off the floor; on this, gymnasts perform a series of dance moves and acrobatic skills.

blind landing: A landing in which the gymnast ends up facing forward, sometimes away from the apparatus, and she cannot see the floor before landing

Comaneci: Named for Nadia Comaneci, the first woman to perform it in competition, this skill is one in which the gymnast swings backward, then lets go of the bar, executes a front flip, and grabs the bar again as she completes the move.

floor: A carpeted surface measuring forty feet square, over springs and wooden boards. Also the term for the only event in which a gymnast performs a routine set to music; the routine is ninety seconds in length, and composed of dance and acrobatic elements.

flyer: A cheerleader who is tossed in the air through the basket toss, to perform jumps, twists, flips, or other stunts, while other cheerleaders form a base for her on the ground

full-in: Two flips in the air with the first flip featuring a 360-degree twist

giant hop full: A skill performed on the uneven bars in which the gymnast swings her outstretched body all the way around the bar. When she reaches the top of the bar, she lets go and goes into a full twist, remaining in handstand position, before catching the bar again.

giant swing: A skill done on the uneven bars that forms the foundation of most other routines, in which the gymnast swings all the way around the bar with straight legs and pointed toes

grips: Strip of leather placed on a gymnast's hand to prevent calluses and allow for a better grip on the uneven bars

handspring: A move in which a gymnast starts on both feet, jumps to a position supporting her body with just her two hands on the floor, and then pushes off to land on her feet again. This can be done forward or backward, and is typically used to start or connect an acrobatic series.

hurkey: A cheerleading jump with one leg bent toward the ground and the other stretched straight out to the side

Junior Elite: The level before Senior Elite, as designated by regulations of the governing body of gymnastics. Junior Elite gymnasts are not allowed to compete in the Olympics.

layout: A maneuver completed in the air with hands held against the body and a pencil-straight overall position; flipping can be forward or backward, and the move ends with the gymnast standing on both feet again.

optional routines: Routines performed on the floor in gymnastics where the gymnast is able to make up her own combination of dance elements, acrobatic skills, tumbling passes, and release skills, as well as choose her own music. The lower levels in gymnastics often require compulsory routines, where all gymnasts perform the same combination of skills, so optional routines are a sign of the gymnast's growth and development.

pike: A position in which the body is bent double at the hips, with legs straight and toes pointed

release skill: Any skill performed on the uneven bars that requires the gymnast's hands to leave the bar before returning to it, usually after a twisting or flipping skill has been executed

ring leap: A leap in which one of the gymnast's legs is stretched out in front of her, and the other bent behind her, with her toes touching the back of her head

round-off: A move that begins like a cartwheel, but in which the legs swing together overhead, and the gymnast finishes facing in the opposite direction

sheep jump: A move in which the gymnast jumps into the air, throws her head back until it touches her feet for a split second, and then returns to a straight-body position to land on both feet

stalder work: Named after male gymnast Josef Stalder, these kind of skills are completed on the uneven bars. The gymnast begins in a handstand

and moves as if to complete a giant swing, but on the upswing pikes her body and straddles her legs before returning to a straight position at the top of the bar.

still rings: One of the six apparatuses in men's artistic gymnastics. Two rings are suspended from cables, and the gymnast must use them to perform a series of strength maneuvers, holding himself high off the ground, while controlling the movement of the rings, which are meant to remain as still as possible.

tuck: A position in which the knees are folded in toward the chest at a ninety-degree angle, with the waist bent, creating the shape of a ball

tumbling passes: A series of connected acrobatic moves required in a floor-exercise routine

twist: A rotation of the body around the horizontal and vertical axes. Twisting is completed when a gymnast is flipping simultaneously, performing both actions at the same time in the same element. Twisting elements are typically named for the number of rotations completed (e.g.: a half twist is 180 degrees, or half a rotation; a full twist is 360 degrees, or a full rotation; and a double twist is 720 degrees, or two complete rotations).

uneven bars: (often, just "bars") one of four apparatuses in women's artistic gymnastics. Bars features the apparatus on which women perform mostly using their upper-body strength. This event consists of two rails placed at an uneven level; one bar acts as the high bar and the other as the low bar. Both bars are flexible, helping the gymnast to connect skills from one to the other.

vault: A runway of approximately eighty feet in length, leading to a springboard and a padded table at one end. The gymnast runs full speed toward the table, using the springboard to launch herself onto it; she then pushes off with her hands, moving into a series of flips and/or twists before landing on the mat behind the table.

Yurchenko vault: A vaulting move that begins with a round-off onto the springboard, followed by a back handspring onto the table; the gymnast then pushes off into a series of flips and/or twists before landing on the mat. This style vault was named after Soviet gymnast Natalia Yurchenko.